COBALT CITY CHRISTMAS

Timid Pirate Publishing, 2010

Direct all orders to:
Timid Pirate Publishing
509 N. 85th St. #14,
Seattle, WA 98103

www.timidpirate.com

ISBN 978-0-9830987-1-3 Printed in the United States of America
Timid Pirate Printing: November, 2010
Limited Edition: November, 2009

COBALT CITY CHRISTMAS
Table of Contents

Other adventures in the Cobalt City Universe:

Chanson Noir*

Cobalt City Blues

Greetings from Buena Rosa*

Ride Like the Devil*

Cobalt City Timeslip

* Timid Pirate Editions forthcoming in 2011.

INTRODUCTION

Set in the fictional metropolis of Cobalt City on the New England coast, this anthology features both original characters (Devil Cat and Imp, the Nutcracker) as well as shared universe characters from the Protectorate and beyond. The shared world of Cobalt City emerged out of transient role-playing games with friends, but has taken on greater depth, longevity and richness, as well as a new mission: to bring in more contributors and readers. All readers are invited to submit to our annual anthologies, growing and developing the unique environment of Cobalt City.

No special advance reading is necessary to enjoy the stories contained herein. However, if your interest is piqued and you want to know more about the heroes of the Protectorate and more about Cobalt City, check out timidpirate.com for background information and to pick up any of the novels or anthologies from Timid Pirate Publishing.

Christmas is a stressful time for everyone. Now imagine the holidays as a super-hero in Cobalt City. Oh and add to that normal stress the fact that you're a part of the cape and cowl community, charged with keeping the city safe. That was the task taken up by a select group of Seattle area speculative fiction authors. We hereby present a series of tales that show what it is to be a super-hero during Christmas time.

Enjoy your time in the city!

Nathan Crowder

SILENT KNIGHTS: TOYS

Nathan Crowder

"Ducks?" Stardust said over the Protectorate comm-link. "Please tell me you aren't serious?" He arced through the icy winter sky above downtown Cobalt City on his way to the harbor, a golden nimbus from his blue and gold power armor flowing in his wake.

"So many giant rubber ducks it will make your heart hurt," Gallows assured him, balanced on a bobbing perch in the harbor itself, leather jacket whipping in the cold wind off the river. "I'm on the back of one now and I'd say it's twenty feet if it's an inch."

"How are they armed?" Stardust asked, fearing the worst. He could see the harbor across the river, over in Quayside. The water was jammed with bobbing yellow shapes, menacing the cargo ships docked there. Even worse, if the ducks turned their attention to the nearby bridge packed with early evening Christmas shoppers, they might be able to do enough damage to bring it down, leading to enormous casualties. It was madness. But that was what Stardust had come to expect from Maiden China.

"Each duck is equipped with fifty caliber chain-guns in the head and mini-rockets in wing bays." Archon piped in from the deck of the Immer Essen, a cargo tanker out of Hamburg docked in Quayside. He consulted the mini-computer in his hand, his insulated spandex jacket and fingerless gloves letting him ignore the cold almost entirely. "There are approximately two hundred of them running on hardwired directives, rather than radio commands. Hacking their programming won't be an option like it was with the Boom Boom Babies from last month," he said.

"Approximately two hundred?" Velvet replied from her perch on the bridge, where she oversaw the ducky blockade. Her armored, midnight blue cloak whipped around her as she clung athletically to the frosted girders with her iron-gloved fist. "You're usually more precise than that."

"Two hundred and fourteen," Archon said. "I was not aware you wanted exact numbers. Regardless, I see no sign of Maiden China herself or a radio signal to the ducks that I can triangulate. I'm not going to be much help here."

Floating in the air above the duck armada, Stardust let loose with a barrage from his bracers. Golden bolts of high energy lanced from the icy night sky, turning one attack duck into yellow slag. "Do we have any backup on the way?"

"Stardust, this is Tanya at the dispatch desk," their on-duty communications staff answered. "The big board shows Worm Queen two minutes from your location. Dr. Shadow and Mister Gray are engaged with the Ghost of Christmas Past in the Cannonade, Knockabout is engaged downtown with the Little Match Girl serial arsons and Wild Kat is on stakeout in Regency Heights to try and stop Victor Cross from assassinating Senator Finlay. Would you like me to activate any reserves?"

Stardust thought about his options. There were only two reservists, the young archer, Huntsman and the psychic Libertine. Neither of them were particularly heavy hitters. He would have really preferred the wide-scale gravity and kinetic control of Knockabout, but the serial arsons in downtown were a higher priority. And Worm Queen had enough of a wild card factor that they might be able to control the ducks here—with some luck. "No, save the reserves for Knockabout," he said.

"If I may," Archon interjected, "I think that the ducks are diversion to keep us busy while Maiden China achieves her true goal. I have a few ideas where she might be and Gallows and I aren't going to be much help for you here…"

Dozens of high-caliber chainguns cut loose on Stardust, filling the air around him with lead and a flashing golden nimbus as his force field stopped the bullets. "Sic'em, Archon. Tell her 'Hi' from me." Stardust said as he fired off a chain burst from his gauntlets. Three ducks exploded in gouts of orange flame and the smell of gunpowder and burning rubber.

"I make out a group of about twenty or so heading for the central bridge support," Velvet announced. "I'll slow them down, but I might need some backup when you get here, Worm Queen."

"I'm ninety seconds out," the mistress of squirmy, extra-dimensional allies confirmed. "Meet you at the bridge."

With back-up assured, Velvet launched herself off the bridge in a high arc. She used her cloak to guide her as she sliced through the icy air towards the lead duck. The wind whistled past her cowl in the darkness and she willed her teeth to not chatter against the cold. When she was thirty feet from her target, she released her grip on the cloak edge, allowing it to flip up behind her and slow her descent slightly. Velvet used the time to retrieve two small sticky charges from her utility belt and arm them. She landed hard on the back of the lead duck, driving it deeper into the murky waters with the force. The rubber surface stretched and gave and at the depth of the parabola, Velvet slapped the two sticky charges on the duck wings above the mini-rocket bays. The combination of rubber landing surface and water pressure vaulted her off the duck's back as surely as a trampoline and she used the momentum to flip through the air to the back of another duck.

The sticky charges went off, triggering the charges in the mini-rockets beneath the wings. The resulting POP POP POP exploding behind Velvet brought a smile to her face, as well as sinking the lead duck. On the back of her second target, she calmly punched through the wing bays with her iron fist clad in midnight blue velvet, disabling the wings one by one.

When other ducks in the flotilla opened fire with their machine guns, Velvet raised her armored cloak, feeling the ballistic fabric buckle and heave with each bullet. Sparing a glimpse around the cloak, she picked another target. Velvet took a breath and vaulted high through the stream of flying lead to the temporary safety of another duck's back. She let down her guard only long enough to disable this third duck and check on the one she had just left, now so pocked with large holes that it was slipping beneath the river. She was pleased to see that these cheery yellow menaces were not immune to friendly fire. She was doubly pleased that it took close to seven seconds for the machine guns to re-target her. That was plenty of time. She vaulted from back to back, disabling rocket packs, lingering just long enough to draw several bursts of machine gun fire to further damage her short-term platform.

Velvet had fatally disabled ten of the ducks before Worm Queen arrived with the signature cry of "Worms, to ME!"

In her headset, Velvet heard Anna Lyta, Cobalt City's enigmatic Worm Queen. "Hey, Velvet! Sorry for the delay. You're going to want to jump straight up first chance you get. The cavalry is here."

Looking up, Velvet spotted Worm Queen riding on the back of a thick, twisting pale orange worm that had to be close to 20' long. Clad in her signature black spandex body suit decorated up the legs and torso with entwined multi-colored worm shapes, the Worm Queen extended a hand to Velvet. The cloaked warrior leapt and caught the proffered hand, swinging up onto the back of the transport. She found it disturbingly warm between her thighs. It took a second for her to realize this was most likely intentional. If a person could customize their ride to patrol the city, why not one with seat warmers?

Seconds later, there was a disturbance in the water as several dozen translucent shapes slid from beneath the ducks, wrapping around them. At first, it appeared to Velvet that they were worms, trying to pull the ducks below the surface, but then she saw the large yellow shapes distorting beneath her.

"I thought of using water worms to pull them under, but I couldn't be certain that they could hold them under long enough to short out the firing mechanisms," Worm Queen said idly. "So I went another way."

"What kind of worms did you..." Velvet began, vaguely horrified as the giant yet still strangely cute duckies warped and melted in the waves. One turned an accusing eye in their direction as it went down.

"Oh," Worm Queen said, looking over her shoulder at Velvet with a half smile, "Worms that eats rubber."

"They have those?"

Worm Queen shrugged. The last of the ducks that had separated to attack the bridge sank beneath the dark surface of the river. "Apparently so."

They turned back to help Stardust, but found only stragglers. The armored industrialist had laid into his ducky attackers with a vengeance and the harbor was lit with as many as fifty flaming yellow hulks floating aimlessly upon the water. "Maybe we should just let him work this out," Velvet suggested.

"Wow...he and Maiden China just really don't get along, do they!?" Worm Queen whistled low.

"She's his arch nemesis," Velvet answered. "He's a billionaire tech developer with strong feeling on fair trade practices and quality control. Their views on capitalism and industry couldn't be more different. Let's just hope that Archon and Gallows get to her before Stardust does."

"So noted," Worm Queen said, directing her rubber-eating worms to pick away at the stragglers and already disabled ducks. "I wonder how the boys are doing?"

"Okay, location three – batteries. Everybody out," Gallows said as he and Archon appeared on the steel mesh catwalk of one of Starcom's Cobalt City manufacturing pods. Already they had checked a warehouse and an assembly factory for the cell phones made by Stardust's subsidiaries. The other two locations were a bust, but it only took twenty seconds in each place to make sure they were clear.

Archon checked his mini-computer, tapping twice with his stylus before sliding it back into the case at his hip. The overlay of the building appeared on the miniature screen he wore in his left eye like a contact lens. This was the first test run of his Heads Up Display and he was secretly pleased that it was working well. Having a HUD kept his hands free and should be most useful, provided no one punched him in the eye. The Protectorate's resident expert in just about everything rarely let himself get hit, but he didn't know how the lens would hold up to that kind of direct pressure.

"Search drill one," Archon whispered to his old friend. They worked well with the Protectorate team, but their long familiarity led to an advantage in rhythm and split-second understanding.

Gallows nodded and began blinking to the security checkpoints around the building and the exterior fence looking for signs of intrusion. He reported back via communicator before Archon had finished sliding to the factory floor. "Gate camera is disabled and the two guards are unconscious. I see a truck parked at the loading dock from here. Oh and she had a security drone in place at the gate. It's gone now."

"Gone where?" Archon whispered as he moved silently towards the loading dock.

"An abandoned and flooded copper mine in Chile," Gallows said with his usual dry delivery. "Why do you think she picked this place to target?"

"They make the batteries for Starcom cell phones here. They go through intensive quality checks before being shipped out, but when they're installed, they don't get the same attention. One of Maiden China's front companies received a significant shipment two days ago. I suspect that this shipment was tainted batteries she intends to mix in with the Starcom batteries. They are designed to fail and will cause a massive recall of the phones, not to mention untold injury when they fail catastrophically."

"She really doesn't like Jaccob, does she? Is she like an ex or something?"

"An ex what?" Archon whispered. Gallows didn't answer, which was just fine. The loading bay area was within view now and he could clearly see Maiden China with a half dozen henchmen making the switch on crates of batteries. The Chinese technophile was dressed in classically inspired layered armor in cinnabar red, but instead of laminated bamboo, this armor was micro-thin metal, strengthened by a magnetic field. The sword on her belt heated to almost nine hundred degrees Fahrenheit at the press of a button. There were likely to be a reserve of high-tech drones lying in wait to attack. "Pinpoint my location and port in right behind me. I can deal with the Maiden and her flunkies, but if she has a drone swarm, I'd rather be prepared."

"I'm on it," Gallows whispered from behind him.

Archon toggled the controls in his jacket to change the fabric's color, mimicking the beige and gray of the loading dock walls. Thus moderately camouflaged, he snuck down the side of the bay. He was upon two of the lackeys with lightning speed, dropping each with a precision strike to nerve clusters in their torso.

Leg sweeps and two more precision blows dropped two more guards before anyone else could react. The two remaining assistants dropped their crates of batteries and reached for guns. At a calculated, safe distance Maiden China drew her sword.

Two fingers in a nerve cluster under the arm paralyzed one guard temporarily, while two fingers from Archon's other hand drove the wind from the final guard's lungs. A swift finishing blow to their temples laid them out, leaving just Archon and Maiden China standing in the loading bay.

A cloud of whirring mini-copters, each armed with poison darts took flight from the girders above them. But as soon as they made their presence known, they vanished again without warning. Archon suspected they were at the bottom of an abandoned mine in Chile.

"I was expecting Jaccob," the bitter technophile said in crisp, perfect English, ignoring the disappearance of her mechanical defenders. She gripped her sword tightly before her and heat illusions rippled off the white blade. Only ten feet – three good steps, would put them within close combat range.

"I am a master of fourteen martial arts. I have calculated nine ways to defeat you before you even advance upon me. As for Stardust, he sends his regards," Archon smiled, "But he didn't want to encourage you by showing up himself. This little crush has gone on long enough, don't you think?"

With a roar and a reckless lunge that could only come from forgetting all training, Maiden China plunged the superheated sword towards Archon's heart. He hesitated, pivoted lightly to the left and the white-hot blade passed within inches of his breast. Calmly, he tapped a nerve cluster in Maiden China's wrist and the blade fell to the ground just past his left foot, sticking into the concrete with a hiss.

"I have now calculated thirty-seven ways to defeat you," Archon said flatly.

She wheeled backward quickly to regain her composure. She could not have anticipated Gallows having teleported two of her unconscious guards directly behind her feet. She fell hard, striking her head upon a discarded crate of batteries. The blow stunned her into a sudden sleep.

"Make that thirty-eight ways," Gallows said from the shadows of the factory floor. He sauntered into the loading bay to survey the damage. The sword had started cooling and the cocky teleporter crouched to get a better look at it. "Can I keep the sword?"

"No."

"I'm just saying, Christmas is right around the corner and if you hadn't gotten anything for me yet, this sword would be just fine," Gallows pushed, not looking up at his friend's stern expression.

"I got your present in June," Archon said. "Now, let's get these sorry individuals to the police and then see if the rest of the Protectorate needs help. It's shaping up to be a busy holiday season."

HOME FOR CHRISTMAS

Nicole Burns

The sky made all of the difference. It was wild and alone, but not lonely; it was too vast and alive to be lonely. The best skies happened in the darkness of the early winter mornings, when the wind riding on high drove the clouds to ambition and they tried to swallow the moon. But when the winds were like that, high and domineering, the clouds were too shallow to achieve their goal and rather than obscuring the silvery orb they found themselves exposed by her, illuminated from within for the world to see.

She stood poised on the sidewalk, reveling in the wildness of the midnight sky while her hair blew damply across her face. The silver light and the skyscrapers mingled to cast eerie shadows across the shining pavement. The spectacle gave her a welcome pause. As she took a deep breath of the cold winter air, an alien scent began to crowd the angry and forlorn scents indigenous to Cobalt City, breaking her out of the moment and back into reality. It carried with it a whispered reminder.

"…nexus."

A pigeon out late cocked its iridescent head at her, yellow eyes knowing. A sound burst suddenly upon her eardrums, not a surprise, building rapidly to a roar – and a softer sound, the slight scraping twang of metal passing swiftly over metal, sharp and subtle below the roar. She smiled and stepped into the night.

Sylvia Keller had grown quieter with the passing of the years. Her old friends would never have believed such a thing possible, but they had long since drifted off or faded from her life. An only child of traveling parents, she was no stranger to loneliness. It was with a feeling of inevitability that she experienced the passing of first her mother, then her father a scant three years later.

Her job was no help. She had embraced her college degree in accounting and rather too quickly found a position in a large company that imported massive amounts of wholesale textiles. The raw bolts of fabric were bound for clothing manufacturers that would then label their products "Made in America." The company was huge and employed a dozen low-level assistants, analysts and number crunchers. The work was hard enough to keep them occupied and offered large quantities of overtime rather than taking on new positions. The pay was just enough to keep them until they could find better and turnover was extremely high. Sylvia never became part of that turnover statistic and the gray corporate miasma crept over her, inducing a sickly pallor and a meekness that never quite went away.

The holiday season invaded her life every year like heavy smog, insidious and unsettling. Christmas in the city was a time of simple endurance. The gaudy decorations, the packed stores and the tinny music emanating from cheap speakers combined with the ebb and flow of jostling and joyous crowds. Although she no longer consciously recognized it, she felt a little emptier every time they rushed upon her. The memories that struck her now and again during the season brought a wistful longing: sitting with her parents in the rosy glow of a crackling fire after a holiday dinner, pausing in her rush on campus when the clock tower's ancient chimes rang out with melody at the hands of an earnest music student, catching sight of a tiny but perfect snowflake as it settled on the dark paint of a car.

They all served to make the emptiness deeper.

Early morning and late evening alike, when she walked through the deserted streets to or from work and occasionally wondered whether there was something better, the emptiness was the worst. The city was always the same to her tired, overworked eyes; gray and dreary, as though it had no time to care about its inhabitants. The modern city clock struck hollow synthesized tones every hour on the hour, filling her ears with the dull sound of loss or warning.

The holidays, Simon thought morosely. Ah, the holidays. He swept down the avenue, a tall gray man with hat pulled low over bandaged face, thick-rimmed glasses and collar turned against the cold. Except of course, that he was no longer a man. Conscious of every mote of ash that comprised his current form and still somewhat self-conscious about it, it was rare to see him simply walking down the streets in the middle of the day. "So what am I doing?" he muttered aloud.

Even in the chill of winter, when muffled faces were routine against the freezing wind and bits of sleet, people unconsciously parted to make way for him. The joie-de-vivre that whipped society into a frenzy of shopping and laughter stilled a little. It washed around him without coming close enough to touch, leaving a little bubble of quiet for him to walk in. Bother, he thought, turning down a mercifully unpopulated alleyway. The holiday sounds faded rapidly behind him.

Simon was no longer strictly corporeal, but his deeper animal instincts were still good. Good enough that the movement behind him, subtle and silent though it was, put him instantly on alert. "What do you want," he asked, his voice purposely deep and desiccated enough to give an ordinary mugger serious pause. He knew that this was no ordinary mugger, of course. It never was.

Simon didn't need to turn around to see the shadows unwind and a bright, shrewd pair of eyes gaze at him. A distinct moment of hesitation, or possibly cold assessment, fixed them both in place: the ashy form with its back turned to a black lightless bulk obscured but not hidden by a restaurant dumpster. Then the tension ebbed palpably. The shadow grunted, oddly familiar, picked something up off of the ground and emerged into the alley.

For a moment, Simon just stared. The figure grunted again and then growled in a voice that he would not have recognized without the visual, "You could turn around. I know you don't have to. I'm just sayin'."

There was really nobody she could tell when it started. It didn't affect her job efficacy or her ability to pay the rent or climb

11

the stairs to her room. Once one of her co-workers had seen her turn pale and asked if she was all right, but body language clearly indicated after her vague nod that it was not a time for conversation. So nobody else knew.

Sylvia was teetering on the brink of... something.

It wasn't a completely alien experience. Ever since she was a young child, she had experienced moments of very clear, strong déjà vu. She would turn a corner, or hear a phrase and be struck by the immediate certainty that she had not only experienced that exact moment before, but also knew unequivocally what was going to happen next. She had also learned to discount the eerie feeling. The thing that was going to happen next, the thing that she knew would absolutely happen next, never actually did happen. Reality held itself aloof from her odd premonitions.

But lately, that relatively mild and innocuous sense had developed into something rather more disturbing. The first time it happened, it was pretty mild. The déjà vu was accompanied by a faint sensation of nausea and disorientation, making her pause as she walked home. For a moment, it seemed as though the world was shifting around her, from the angle of the lights to the temperature of the air. Then it simply wasn't and everything was just as it had been. Accustomed to ignoring her déjà vu, she had breathed deep of the crisp morning air and moved on.

But it happened again and again, with stronger impact on her physical well-being and stability. She started to have nightmarish premonitions; she knew with every fiber of her being that something terrible was about to happen. The sensation left her gasping and leaning on some nearby stable point for support, a thick metallic smell filling her nostrils and her stomach roiling like an angry cauldron. She went to her doctor, who listened to her feeble attempt to explain the phenomenon with a condescending half-smile. He simply agreed with her that it "was odd," and prescribed better hydration and some anti-nausea medication. She drank plenty of water and tucked the medication away, knowing it wouldn't help and lived around the strange interruptions as best she could.

Until the day when her world was literally rocked by it.

The bus station was a mass of contrasts. The elegant modern architecture was eclipsed by the unheeding hum of everyday commuters and the smell that public spaces in Cobalt City acquired with time and regular use. She left work early enough to avoid the afternoon rush; still, there were plenty of people in the station while she waited for her commuter bus to arrive. They were commuters like her, interspersed with a couple of transients as usual and they had no time for a diminutive woman who suddenly paled and leaned against a pillar for support.

Sylvia closed her eyes briefly, but it only made her premonition that much more clear. She hoped the disorientation would dissipate quickly. Then she actually felt the earth moving under her feet and she opened her eyes again.

"No," she whispered in disbelief as she saw the beginning of her vision becoming reality. The people around her had paused in the moment before panic sets in and the solid pillar itself was trembling like a leaf under her hand. She knew that the force of the quake would burst the blacktop. She could almost see the great slabs jutting from the former roadway, the busses tipped and tossed like matchsticks and the people in a panic of fear rushing madly about trying to escape the death trap that the station had become and the entire city in chaos.

Earthquakes strike almost instantaneously and are usually over before people actively realize what is going on. As the blacktop cracked and began to shift, as people fell to the floor, Sylvia felt as though the epicenter was not deep under the earth as it must be, but inside her own body, bursting to escape. Her immediate and unconscious response was denial. That transitioned swiftly into a conscious effort of will, without her really understanding the reason for it. She denied the right and ability of the earthquake to change and re-shape her world. She forced herself to believe that this could not be.

"No!" she repeated, her throat raw with defiance and fear. For a split second, the world was silenced, as though in response to her cry.

Then someone near her whispered, hissed a word she would learn to understand and dread. "Nexus…"

And the blacktop was whole as though it had never been rent. Slowly the people around her picked themselves up off of the ground. They looked at one another as people granted a sudden reprieve often do, taking stock of themselves and their surroundings. Not one noticed Sylvia, suddenly exhausted but still holding tight to her pillar, having forgotten to let go although the danger of a fall had passed.

That evening, a local news anchor reported a magnitude 8.6 earthquake with an epicenter located where no fault had been found before, directly below Cobalt City. Fortunately, the anchor simpered, her plasticine hair shining and too-perfect, the quake had struck so deep that absolutely no damage and no injuries had been reported. Sylvia blanched as the experts started their two-bit analyses, hastily pushed away her small half-finished dinner and scurried off to bed.

"There," said the Snowflake that Simon really didn't know at all. Oh, the face was right and the stature and general aura of crankiness. But the matte black battle-armor and the cold efficiency with which this evolved panda spoke and moved were alien to him. "The shockwave was met there." He pointed with a stubby, thick finger to the well-populated South Station, a bustling hub of transportation that housed not only a bus section, but also light rail and airport shuttles. Then he frowned, glaring at the device Simon had seen him retrieve in the alley. "Not met," he mumbled. "Repulsed. Actively."

"And what, precisely, does that mean?" Simon asked. He wanted Snowflake to speak more, although he knew damn well it wasn't in his nature. Simon had dealt with the Protectorate's counterparts from an alternate reality before and had learned caution. This Snowflake, he felt instinctively, was no competent misfit sidekick. He was too concentrated and radiated purpose. Which could mean he was a hero, or could mean something much worse.

Safety inspectors still swarmed the Station, almost as thick as the winking white Christmas lights. They were busy roping off and examining the structure to see how it had weathered the quake. A cold winter rain had begun and it was a relief to step out of it and into a shelter. Simon always had to focus a little harder on keeping up appearances in the rain.

"It means," said the alternate Snowflake, the device that measured God-only-knows what away, "that the Nexus is near."

He stole a sideways glance at Simon that the ash-gray man did not miss, although he didn't turn his head. "It also means your world has within it a creature whose actions can consciously affect other realities. Your own nexus. Your very reality is in grave danger because of it."

Simon didn't bother to conceal his skepticism. The panda had reduced his story to the bare essentials, speaking in abrupt bursts as he supposedly used the small, complex meter to track the source of the disturbance. He claimed to come from a parallel dimension, rather far away in the vast spiral of alternate realities that had been described to Simon by another mysterious personage not nearly long enough ago. He was searching for a man who, by nature, was capable of affecting multiple realities near his own. This arch-villain was using his abilities like sonar, initiating violent changes in reality that spread though the spiral like ripples in a pond after someone had thrown a rock. Snowflake had simply called the man "the Nexus." Not satisfied with his own ability to affect reality, this Nexus was searching through neighboring dimensions for a counterpart, someone who could help him to build the world, the reality, he aspired to.

"But how do these changes help him locate the other nexus?" Simon asked.

"The same way they help me," Snowflake replied.

"Are you being deliberately cryptic?"

He sighed. "Look, I'm not used to having to explain myself, all right? It's like this. The Nexus makes a change in reality; you got that? He can feel it, direct it and it moves away from him in a sort of dimensional shockwave. Sometimes it rides against rocks and he gets a mild bounce-back.

"But if the wave runs into another nexus, that nexus doesn't like being messed with. It pushes back, to keep reality the way it likes it, see? And that counter-wave ripples back through realities, negating or lessening the effects of the first wave, until finally it reaches the first Nexus. He feels it like you feel the wake of a speedboat. It's directional – you can tell where a wake is coming from, right? So he moves closer. And does it again. You got it?"

The small dark eyes were intense and irritated as the panda-man stared at him, but Simon was somewhat reassured. He had heard Snowflake – the Snowflake that belonged to this reality – become frustrated, down tools and explain a mechanical concept in precisely this manner.

"Sonar," the panda continued when Simon didn't reply. "Bats. Er, submarines and stuff."

"And that meter, that device you're carrying, it detects these dimensional waves as well."

"Yeah. And it's better than his natural sense, see, because we've learned how to measure the ripples in reality. But we can't make 'em and if we could, we wouldn't, so we have to wait for the Nexus to do it."

"We? You and Manuel?" Simon realized belatedly that he had somehow touched on a sore spot. The panda's jaw clenched and his mouth tightened. Deliberately he turned and without another word strode into the Station, working his way down the levels while consulting the meter. With an ashy sigh, Simon followed behind.

Sylvia called in sick the next day. She knew she couldn't face work, much less concentrate on it, even though she had already begun to rationalize her experience. She was stressed, she thought; too much work during the busy season. She hadn't gotten enough fresh air lately. Clearly the stress had been gradually building up and she had ignored the warning signs. If she wanted to stay sane, she needed rest and maybe some light exercise.

She woke early and began the reassuringly mundane task of cleaning the apartment. The smell of detergent and the smattering of bubbles under the sponge as she cleaned the kitchen was refreshing. While dusting, she stopped for the first time in ages to really look at the photo on the shelf of her parents. It was her favorite photo, taken just a year or two after they were married. They were smiling and relaxed as some friend took their picture in a snowbound park. Her mother wore bright red knitted mittens and a warm black woolen coat. Her father was in a dark jacket with red and white diagonal stripes, his hair exposed to the cold and his brown eyes sparkling behind thick glasses. Together, they held a heart made of packed snow.

"I'll do something today," she said aloud, still holding the duster. "I'll have a nice lunch and go to the park. It'll be good for me." Nobody answered, but her apartment seemed cheered by her voice.

She finished cleaning hastily, planning for once to enjoy the festive holiday sights and sounds. Then she unpinned her short black hair, cleaned up her glasses and changed into her best skirt and a sweater. Her reflection in the mirror still seemed a little wan, so she cheered it up with a little pair of festive cloisonné earrings and a splash of cold water. Then she wrapped up in a cozy scarf and hat, put on a long warm coat and her purse and tucked her hands into the pockets after closing her door behind her.

The weather was dank and disappointing. It was a little too early for winter snows and the precipitation fell as cold and uninspired rain, mindlessly soaking anything that wasn't fully waterproof. Without the rampant commercial holiday lights, wreaths and decorations, Cobalt City would have been gray sky on gray skyscrapers on gray pavement – an artist's monochromatic palette of gloom. She found it almost absurdly simple to stay under the near-continuous city eves, but dodging the rain and traffic wasn't what she had in mind for de-stressing. She found her stomach curling unasked into an uncomfortable knot as the noise and bustle of the city intruded on her calm. Her heart rate increased perceptibly as she realized that her stress hadn't lifted.

A warm café with an open door beckoned and she darted through the streets to meet it. Ordering a cup of coffee alone was no substitute for a hot drink with a friend, but the comfortable neutral tones of the walls and the warm reds and vibrant greens of the holiday décor were carefully calculated to convey welcome. They helped put her back at ease, as did the friendly smiles of the baristas. She wrapped her hands around the warm cup, leaning back into the slightly worn fabric of a small, upholstered chair. The rain seemed more alive framed by the window. Heavy drops gathered and sparkled on the eves and twinkled briefly in the holiday lights before splashing onto the waiting pavement. Sylvia sighed with contentment, finally feeling the knot unwind.

She finished her coffee slowly, letting her mind drift. Warmed and relaxed, she rose reluctantly from the comfortable chair, returned her cup to the bussing station and stepped back refreshed into the world. The rain had stopped and across the street was the smallish, manicured park in the midst of town, locally known as the Square. The perfectly mowed lawn sparkled where it had not been stepped on. Sylvia stopped for a moment under a tree, smiling around her. Save for a couple of harried passers-by, she was the only visitor and she wondered how long it had been since she had really stopped to look around in the city.

She had buried her hands in her coat and was strolling toward the fountain when she heard the whisper again, uncanny and certainly not human. "Nexus…" Her fists tightened as she strained her eyes to find the source. It was the fountain itself, thousands of tiny droplets whispering to her and as she stared she heard it again, clearly: "nexus." So she was not surprised to be struck by nausea once more. The clarity of the vision startled her, though and a cry escaped through her clenched teeth. She saw the lawn she had just crossed, the little city-friendly trees and the cobblestone roundabout, all were uprooted and sucked into the fountain, swallowed by waters colder, darker and more pervasive than they should have been. Loamy earth sagged and rippled into mud; the concrete barriers that held the fountain in crumbled into obscurity as the dark shoreline expanded and spread like a disease.

"It hasn't happened yet," she thought. Then with fierce rebellion, "It *won't* happen." The hiss of the fountain was a roar in her ears, but she set herself against it and whatever impetus - whatever entity, she realized, was behind it. Angrily she pictured the park as it was, the park as it would still be, cobblestones and trees and lawn in their place, unmarred by the rush of mud and willed it to be.

When she opened her eyes she was on the ground, the wet and slippery lawn slightly torn up beside her where her shoe had skidded on the way down. Her disorientation was extreme and her breast heaved with spent effort and emotion; it would have taken very little provocation for her to disgorge the remains of her coffee right there on the ground. The harsh metallic scent that she associated with the episode easily overwhelmed the smell

18

of freshly bruised grass. But that was all minor. She knew now that there was a consciousness guiding the horrifying premonitions and she knew it was aware of her and most importantly, she knew she could stop it for now. "Nexus," the fountain murmured again, but the whisper was distant and benign.

Sylvia did not really see the tall stranger who helped her to her feet, although she thanked him politely. He hurried to catch up to his stout companion who was moving determinedly toward the fountain. In the daze that follows epiphany, Sylvia made her way back home, a few stray motes of ash clinging unnoticed to her hand.

"We were close, this time," Snowflake said hoarsely as Simon caught up to him.

"How did you know it would be here?" he asked, stepping lightly to join his companion on the cobblestone roundabout that surrounded the little fountain.

"I didn't." His furry companion contemplated the sparkling rain-freshened water, meter hanging loosely at his side. "Sometimes you're just lucky." He heaved a sigh and looked again at the readings on his meter. "He's getting much closer to this dimension. If we could just find your nexus…"

"Should we talk to the people at the park?" asked Simon.

The panda shook his head lugubriously. "I don't think he can target the dimensional waves that closely. Your nexus could be anywhere in the city, or even outside the city. Like I said, we just got lucky." He closed his eyes and put a paw to his head.

"You should get some rest. Have you slept at all since you got here?"

"You're not my mother," growled the panda. Then he opened his eyes and squinted at his companion. "Sorry," he said, not particularly sincere. "I guess I *could* use some coffee, if you know a place around here. And maybe a taco."

Simon laughed and looked around. "There's a café across the street."

Snowflake drew a few odd glances in the coffee shop, but he ignored them and ordered with surprisingly competent familiarity.

Simon flinched slightly at the upbeat jazz-ish compilation of standard Christmas carols before tuning them out. The wreaths and lights were easier for him to ignore.

They sat down at a table by the window. Simon let the panda-man take a deep draught of the restorative beverage before breaking into his reverie.

"I don't mean to be intrusive," he began, "but it's apparent that you are exhausted and maybe you could use some competent help, if not some rest. In this reality, Cobalt City seems to be a target for a great deal of supernatural activity and a number of us have come together to guard against its downfall. I would be happy to recommend your trouble to the Protectorate…" he trailed off as Snowflake almost shot his coffee through his nose.

"You're part of the Protectorate?" he demanded when the coughing subsided.

"Um, yes, rather," replied Simon, taken aback.

Snowflake glared at him over the paper cup for a long minute. Then he grunted matter-of-factly and took another sip of coffee.

Simon continued, more guardedly. "We have some experts in technology that might be able to replicate your dimensional-wave detection device and we are accustomed to tracking unusual activity. Let me give them a call—"

"No," exploded his companion, in a roar loud enough to attract momentary attention once again from the other customers. Simon looked at him in shocked silence. "No," he repeated in a more reasonable tone, although still clearly agitated. "Don't call your damned Protectorate."

"I do not know what your relationship with Manuel de la Vega and the Protectorate are in your dimension," Simon replied quietly, "but here I consider them both trustworthy and capable. We have been through a great deal together and, as the name implies, have protected this city and world from threats both native to our reality and otherwise."

The panda shook his head again, fiercely. "You don't understand," he snarled.

"Then enlighten me," Simon demanded, leaning back in his chair and crossing his arms.

He had to wait. The panda seemed to be mulling him over, unabashedly fixing him with a wary gaze. He took another deep draught of his coffee and rolled it around for a moment in his mouth, as though ridding himself of a bad taste. Then the intensity retreated back under the gruff demeanor and he sighed heavily enough to ripple the cooling drink.

"Yes," Snowflake said once the liquid had slipped down his throat. "We too had a Protectorate that was all of those things. Manuel was part of it. It was strong." A silent snarl marred his expression briefly. "Trustworthy and capable."

"You'll have to understand, I was not part of the Protectorate. I was – many of us were – support staff. Heroes can't be everywhere and do everything if they don't have proper equipment and backing. We were proud to support them. They went out into the world, sometimes got the crap beaten out of them, usually got the crap beaten out of their equipment and came back to us. And we fixed it and them, not only because it was a job, but because we believed with all of our hearts in what they could and did do." He paused. "We believed in *them*."

"That was before the Nexus. He did not come into his full power all at once. He took long decades to learn about and develop his abilities. At first, the ripples in reality were so small that nobody knew they were there. Reality has a vast and powerful momentum. Throw a rock in a river and you might divert it temporarily, but the river closes around it and rushes off where it was going anyway, right? So the Protectorate and no doubt the generation of heroes that preceded them, were unaware of the source of the growing problems the city faced. They just tackled each incident independently.

"But the Nexus had a purpose, a powerful reason to try to change reality. The ripples grew larger and more improbable and the Protectorate began to detect them. It wasn't long after that, as our reality began to change course perceptibly, that one of them began to put two and two together. They started tracking the incidents, plotting their possible course and origin. They discovered the source. Our heroes cleverly, capably tracked the Nexus down. And because he was a threat to the city, they tried to stop him."

Snowflake stared into his now cold half-cup as though he could escape through it to a better time and place. For a moment, Simon saw regret in the small brown eyes. Then they hardened and the regret was gone, replaced again by a powerful sense of purpose.

"They didn't know how far he had come, how easy it had become for the Nexus to bend reality to his will. Three unsuccessful attempts to capture, incapacitate, or kill. That's all it took. The Nexus decided they were getting in his way. That they were intolerable. They had to change and change is what he is expert at. So when the Protectorate confronted him the fourth time, ready, they thought, to contain him successfully, he was prepared for them. He didn't have to reach far; they were all in the same city block. Reality twisted like a knife in some poor jerk's back."

The panda breathed heavily for a moment, remembering. He swallowed the cold coffee in a single gulp, grimacing.

"It took the rest of us a while to understand what he had done. The Protectorate didn't come home that day, see. They didn't report in. There were no pieces of damaged equipment, no minor wounds for us to take care of. So it wasn't until they started taking their own actions and believe me that didn't take very long in the grand scheme of things, that we learned. The Nexus altered their personalities, reversed their very natures. He turned the heroes of Cobalt City into its most vicious enemies." His eyes, now cold and determined, met Simon's.

"You have to understand," he repeated, an implacable agony underlying the firmness of his words, "We were the *support staff.* We knew them. We knew their weaknesses as well as their strengths, sometimes better. And we still believed in their goal. They would have wanted us to protect the city, even – especially – from them. So," he continued bitterly, "we became the heroes.

"We didn't have a whole lot of time to plan; the former members of the Protectorate were wreaking havoc with everything and everyone. We completely dropped the Nexus. Our hands were full and it could not be helped. We had to stop them somehow. We were all the city had left. We tried to capture them, but..." he trailed off, then looked down, spreading blunt fingers on the Formica tabletop. Simon felt a chill of anticipation creep up his spine.

"I killed Manuel with my own hands," he said, his voice dangerously quiet. "Of the entire Protectorate, two were still alive when I left. Wild Kat and the Huntsman were successfully captured and interred in special cells. We… we tried everything we could, mechanical and magical, physical and especially psychological, to bring them back. Our efforts were in vain. They remembered it, they remembered us, but they were not those people any longer. They just didn't care.

"The Huntsman eventually sank into some kind of brooding, impervious meditation and he was still like that when I left. Wild Kat… you can imagine, I suppose, how she responded to captivity, to no longer being in control. Our psychologists couldn't help her and we couldn't let her go."

His lips tightened. "She lost it. She is completely insane now, prowling her cell like an angry tiger stuck in some Podunk zoo."

"Once the City was safe from the former Protectorate, we started after the Nexus. I suppose I led the charge. I was the most pissed off. The others helped me all they could. We didn't have a name, couldn't bring ourselves to declare one, but after dealing with the Protectorate we weren't support staff anymore. We weren't going to let him get away with it. We learned more about him and when he left, his damned shockwaves still washing over the city from neighboring dimensions, I went after him with everything we had. I've been after him ever since."

The rain had started again as Snowflake spoke and whether it was the changing sky or some other darkness, the lights seemed to dim and the holiday decorations seemed to lose some of their festive air.

Simon cleared his throat, started to speak and subsided. Words seemed to have deserted him.

"When I tell you not to call the Protectorate here," Snowflake mumbled, "it's not just to protect them from harm. I don't imagine your Protectorate is identical to what mine was. But it's probably close enough. One of the things we managed to learn about the Nexus is that he finds it much, much easier to change what he knows well than what is unfamiliar to him." He looked up from his hands again. "Your Protectorate cannot help me."

Sylvia stumbled down the streets, her heart pounding like a jackhammer and her vision swimming occasionally either with nausea or tears. "Paranoid delusions," she thought, but in her heart she knew better. Deep draughts of cold, clean, rain-laden air helped keep her going. She made it to her apartment, lay down on her couch without bothering to remove her wet coat or scarf and closed her eyes. Whether it was the stress or the physical activity or the fresh air, she fell immediately into an uneasy sleep.

Her dreams were punctuated by cityscapes that should have been familiar and for hours she tossed and turned but did not wake. It was as if there were eyes on her and she could not hope to be free of them ever again. Whispers seemed to surround her and she could not tell if they were a facet of her dream, or reality itself trying to wake her.

It was after midnight when she opened her eyes. She was on the floor, several feet away from the couch, huddled tightly against the legs of the coffee table. She got up slowly, removing the coat that had twisted around her like a live thing and feeling the depressions in her arms where the table legs had dug into them. Although she didn't feel at all rested, she was also wide-awake and very aware of her surroundings. The entity was still searching for her.

Without closing her eyes, she could feel changes washing against her, almost like ripples in the bath. She could also feel herself resisting them automatically, pushing back against them. The nausea was nearly gone now, whether because the ripples were tiny or simply because she had grown more accustomed to them. Her acute perception of the premonitions remained. As though she had two different movie screens going, she was able to filter the might-have-beens from the reality she firmly held onto.

Still, in spite of her lack of disorientation, Sylvia was uneasy. Whatever or whomever was out there driving these changes in waves against her was getting closer somehow. At some point she would have to face that.

She turned on the television and a little more of her confidence melted away. The news was as sensationalist as ever, she reminded herself. The blaring stories did not mean an intrusion on reality; Cobalt City was perfectly capable of being strange enough on its own. She flipped the channels. Click; politicians gather argumentatively around a tenement house. Click; uniformed police tackle bank robber in the street. Click; super-heroes Wild Kat and Knockabout deliver menace to society.

She let that story play out, news anchor gesturing dramatically at the scene, which resembled the impact point of a small meteorite. The ripples and premonitions made a strange counterpoint to the story. This which must not happen. That which must not happen. Sylvia put her head in her hands, failing utterly to block out the premonitions. "But I am not a hero," she whispered despairingly to the empty room.

Another large wave nearly submerged her, bringing the nausea and disorientation back full force as the news gave over to insipid holiday commercials. In a moment, from every crack in every sidewalk in the city, from the sewers and drains and inside the plastered walls, a massive upwelling of starving cockroaches would emerge. Too small and numerous to be stoppable, the ravening horde would pour through every surface crack and crevice, devouring all organic material until there was nothing left but writhing black carapaces over steel and concrete. She could feel them moving beneath the city. She could see the devastation they would wreak and hear the millions of screaming voices, human and otherwise, protesting in pain and terror as their still-living flesh was stripped and devoured.

With a gasp she pushed against this change too. There were no ravening hordes, she insisted. She could feel the wave fighting back against her, trying to fix its own version of reality. Then it shifted, coming at her from another angle – the ravening hoards were there, but they parted for her and with a simple gesture she banished them whence they came and they scurried in compliance in the face of her power. Still disoriented, she nonetheless resisted this reality too. There were no masses of insects, obedient or otherwise, save for the population native to the sewers of her city. There was nothing out of the ordinary. She would not have it.

25

"Nexus." The longing whisper echoed through the little room, cancelling the noise from the television. She could almost see something forming before her, as though the darkness itself was watching her. She pushed against that too and was frightened to find that it was not like the waves, it did not simply dissipate in the face of her determination. Still, it did not quite materialize and with another little gasp she turned and fled precipitately out of the apartment and into the night.

"He's close now," the panda said. He touched a button on his belt and the matte black armor buzzed with energy, making him once again the menacing bulk he had been in the alley when Simon met him. "He'll break out any time."

Simon had seen the meter over his companion's shoulder often enough to interpret the flickering lines and colors as increased inter-dimensional activity. "I presume you have a plan once he does break out?"

Snowflake growled audibly but probably without realizing he was doing it. "I fully intend to stop him, yes."

"I presume also," Simon continued dryly, "that I am not part of the plan."

The panda's armor unfolded slightly and a specially fitted helmet and a pair of gauntlets emerged from unassuming spaces in the suit's collar and wrists. He looked the part of a somewhat unconventional super-hero now, short and bulky but tough and encased in black metal. Were it not for the streetlights and the full moon he would be virtually invisible to the naked eye.

"Look, I didn't ask you to hang around, but it's always good to have someone watching your back. I'm glad you're here, sure. But I know what I'm up against and you don't. Just be on the lookout for anything strange, you know?"

Simon felt an ironic smile quirk his lips. "I shall endeavor not to be a hindrance," he murmured. It was fairly evident that the panda was watching his own back and still didn't fully trust him.

At least the street was fairly deserted. They had been tracking the dimensional waves most of the night, the meter buzzing on occasion like an angry hornet and Snowflake had grown more and more tense as the attacks on reality escalated. They were little ones, according to the panda, but very real and likely designed specifically to target the second nexus.

They were standing outside an old but respectable apartment building when the ground shook under them. Simon heard a rustle like millions of tiny legs. For a moment in the darkness he thought he saw the sidewalk crack and begin to crawl with the kind of grossly abundant insect life that brought back unpleasant memories, making him second-guess his restraint in not calling in the Protectorate. Then the threat of crawling masses was gone as if it had never been. A lone, aged specimen, standard city roach about the size of his thumb, emerged slowly from a sewer grate next to them. It rested on the sidewalk, breathing perhaps its last and Simon heard it clearly whisper, "nexus…"

The panda heard it too. He glanced sharply at Simon and then down to where Simon was still looking at the bug. "Get ready," he muttered. The sky brightened as a high wind blew gossamer clouds over the moon. A woman from the apartment building emerged and stood on the sidewalk, the wind whipping her short dark hair. A pigeon blew awkwardly from another building and tumbled to a halt on the sidewalk between them. The city clock began to toll the hour.

Sylvia stood in the night air and breathed deeply. An alien scent reached her nostrils. Across the street, where the shadows cast by the streetlights drew together menacingly, she began to detect movement. Another reality was shaping around her. There was no catastrophic event, but the world was warping around her, responding to her very presence, abiding by her wishes and desires. She could change it. She could protect it from change. She was the center of reality, its guide and guardian. This premonition came in the guise of temptation, but she knew it for what it was.

She shook her head. "No," she whispered. The movement began to resolve into a dark swirling mass. Gradually an eerie, charcoal-black face began to take shape between the streetlights. She squinted, trying to make out details, but there were none yet. The face appeared to be wrapped in black bandages. She wanted to draw back in horror, but could not tear her eyes from it.

Slowly, particle by particle, a pair of thick-rimmed glasses appeared. She did not see the eyes behind them, but she felt them immediately focus on her.

Her panic subsided and with it, the nausea and disorientation. She pushed against the vision, but she also read it closely. She knew that the person projecting it, the person forming just across the street particle by particle, didn't give a damn what happened to this reality. He wanted her. Why she didn't know, but she read the desire and knew it for what it was.

Movement toward her from up the street caught her eye, two figures making their way purposefully toward her, or toward the shadows. She recognized them on a deep and visceral level — heroes, she thought. Here to save the world. From me. Another unwanted premonition rocked her, an angry vision of Cobalt City's high-profile heroes congregating on this spot and being wiped out utterly, shoved out of the way by the bitter tides of deliberate change. Thickly she resisted it; her home would not be the same without heroes. But the other's desire for this change was powerful and she found herself struggling against a much stronger force than had resisted her before. The news story from earlier flashed unasked through her mind and with a glorious tingle of freedom, she understood and repeated her own words, this time with conviction. "I am not a hero."

Once more she pushed against the angry tide, throwing against it all of the will that had grown strong in stark contrast to her frail body. With an effort that would have been impossible five minutes before, she subdued the visions of what might have been and replaced them firmly with the reality that was her own. The black and dusty eyes followed her as a tall figure in an overcoat and pulled-down hat began to coalesce. He was waiting for her. Too late, she thought with a small and wry smile. Too late.

She was the only one who expected the sound that burst suddenly on her eardrums; in fact she had summoned it. The softer sound, the slight scraping of metal passing over metal, was irrelevant and did not concern her, although she felt the displacement of air as a heavy figure pounced where she had been standing a moment before. She was there no longer. Sylvia took a well-timed step into the street, just as an apparently out-of-control souped-up street racer took the corner so fast it nearly ran on two wheels. The brightly colored car righted itself, swerving just so in the street, engine screaming. The flash of headlights was not bright enough to drown out the silver moon as it burst forth from the clouds above her. She didn't see or hear the impact. She just watched the resplendent sky.

The blackened mass forming across the street blew suddenly away as though it had never been. The familiar shape that had been forming chilled Simon to the bones he no longer had and he was relieved to see it go. He turned his attention to his companion only to find he had gone. With an utterly astounding leap that must have been assisted by the armor, Snowflake had launched himself not at the apparition across the street, but at the unassuming girl who had just walked out of her apartment. Belatedly Simon realized that she must have been the nexus they were looking for. Then his heart grew hot as he also realized that large claw-like blades had emerged from Snowflake's gauntlets. The panda was poised curbside, watching in disbelief as a small car with a loud engine and a spoiler that made it look like an oversized teakettle went speeding off into the night.

There was a crumpled form in the road, too still to be alive. Simon rushed to it, unaware in his relative haste that his form blurred as it moved in an unnatural manner. Sure enough, there was the girl – what was left of her. The proximity of Snowflake's gruff voice startled him.

"She knew," he said, gazing down at her.

"You were targeting her, not your Nexus," Simon replied accusingly. He rose. There was nothing left to save. "An innocent."

"Did you see him?" the panda replied. Simon wavered uncertainly, still bothered by what he had seen. Then he nodded, slowly.

"In my reality," Snowflake growled, "Mister Grey was never a part of the Protectorate. No one ever had the opportunity to learn his secrets." The panda shook like a wet dog, letting the gauntlets and helmet slide surreptitiously into his armor, exposing his wrinkled face to the moonlight.

"A black hole on its own can stabilize an entire galaxy. But let another black hole travel close to it and together, their interactions will rip whole galaxies apart. The Nexus is a rogue black hole, hurtling through the universe. I couldn't let him find another like him. And I can't kill him. I've tried." Snowflake met Simon's eyes squarely and then turned to his meter. "Anyway. Your reality is saved. Not by any efforts of my own. He'll probably have to return home for a while and try to detect some new dimensional shockwaves. We will stop him. In time."

Simon frowned at the wreck of a body lying in the street. Then he lifted his head. The old clock tower that had always stood at the center of town started to ring with an old Christmas song he knew, the aged chimes echoing in the cold night air and sweetly singing down the streets. Some university kid up late, playing from yellowed sheet music, he thought. Holiday lights twinkled at him from the shop windows.

Snowflake's armor began to buzz with energy again and he appeared to be setting controls on the hand-held device that had already brought him this far. "Wait," Simon said. The panda stopped and looked at him.

"You could use a cup of coffee and maybe a taco. And perhaps," he continued reluctantly, "perhaps I could give you some pointers…"

Snowflake considered him for a moment, then nodded abruptly. He flipped a switch and the buzzing stopped.

"Come on," Simon said. "Let's get her out of the street and call the proper authorities before we go."

"I know this song," muttered the panda as he stooped in the street to help.

As the chimes rang down the empty streets, a thick blanket of clouds came out of nowhere to cover the moon and it started to snow.

SILENT KNIGHTS: SNOW

Nathan Crowder

Bundled-up shoppers with rosy cheeks made their way through the winter wonderland of twinkling lights, pine bough wreaths, nutcrackers and holly and ivy decorating the shop windows. A thin crust of snow marked which cars had parked prior to the last flurry two hours ago. Edirin Okoloko, better known by the citizens of Cobalt City as the Protectorate's Knockabout, had not left his position on the rooftop of the Hawthorne Building for seven hours now. An arsonist was at large in the city, targeting a chain of struggling toy stores. While the owner of the stores admitted he had hired a firebug for insurance purposes, there were two stores left on the contract and no way to call off the remaining fires. Dealing with the situation required a level of diplomacy that he was particularly well suited for.

A few of Knockabout's colleagues were much better suited for dealing with the fire itself. But the arsonist was the Little Match Girl and her arrest would be a public relations nightmare if handled poorly. Dealing with a ragged, seemingly pre-pubescent girl in a violent manner played poorly in the press, no matter her crimes. The arsonist's pyrokinetic abilities allowed her to start a fire merely by staring at an object long enough, so Knockabout didn't even have the luxury of visibly "catching her in the act."

Knockabout's long vigil paid off. On the street eighty feet below, he saw the familiar dirty sweatshirt hood and box of matchbooks. Even up close, she passed for human with ease despite being at least a few hundred years old, but she still couldn't get it through her head that no one bought boxes of matches on the street anymore. Knockabout waited until his target was in position, peering in the window of Magic Moose

Toys, before he stepped from the roof of the Hawthorne. The sacred metals imbedded within his muscle tissues vibrated as he manipulated the forces of physics around himself and when he landed on the sidewalk, it was as if he had just stepped from the curb. He checked the knot on his red silk tie and adjusted the collar of his black, Perry Ellis suit, fearing it had been disheveled from the winds up above.

"I will give you one chance to come along peacefully," he spoke calmly. His voice pitched low – sacred metal vibrated – and the sound carried directly next to the Match Girl's ear. He was disappointed, yet not ultimately that surprised when she turned to face him with a blaze of anger in her eyes.

Matted red curls framed a too-pale face within the hood. She hissed at him and despite the busy street and sidewalks full of late holiday shoppers, Knockabout heard every word perfectly. "You dare to challenge me, human?"

There was a moment of unexpected warmth as Knockabout felt the temperature of his suit begin to climb to combustion levels. He took her response as an unwillingness to come along quietly. With a barely suppressed smile, he let gravity take its natural course.

There was a reason the three block radius centered on this spot was covered with only a thin crust of snow, rather than the eight inches that had accumulated just beyond that range. Knockabout had been busy while he waited for the Little Match Girl, subtly accumulating the falling snow by re-directing its kinetic energy while holding it free from gravity's embrace. The result had been a not-inconsiderable snowdrift suspended in the darkness several stories above this particular window. While he stepped behind a light pole decorated by faux holly, thus breaking her line of sight, the giant, improvised snowball dropped from the sky, smashing the Little Match Girl flat.

Both foot and auto traffic ground to a halt at the spectacle. Good Samaritans were already beginning to dig out the little girl beneath the drift by the time Knockabout had crossed the street. Ignoring the cold, he plunged a hand through the snow until he found the Little Match Girl's wrist. "I found her!" he said loudly. His booming baritone and confident presence did more to assert that he was in charge of the situation than any recognition as a member of Protectorate.

Only able to ignite what she could see, this centuries old, extra-dimensional Fae fire-starter was powerless beneath the obscuring snow. While the others dug her free, Knockabout retrieved a bauble from his jacket pocket, prepared by Doctor Shadow for just such an occasion. He slipped this cold iron bracelet around the Little Match Girl's wrist and latched it in place. As a member of the Doonda Sidhe, the specially prepared metal would dampen her powers until removed – a task that she could not do on her own. Once she was bound and he was assured that the shoppers would have the stunned arsonist freed soon, Knockabout released his grip and stepped back. An ambulance waited around the corner with a pair of police dressed as med techs ready to finalize the arrest out of the public eye. They could take it from here.

He activated his communicator and contacted central dispatch. Fresh flakes of snow were beginning to fall as he waited. "Tanya, please notify the authorities. The Little Match Girl is contained and ready for pick-up."

"Yes, sir."

"Am I needed elsewhere?" He turned his face up and let the flakes fall towards him from the blackness above. Born and raised in an equatorial African country, this was only his second winter somewhere with snow. He still found the experience a novel adjustment.

"Nothing in your area. You are now on standby," the dispatcher confirmed. "Are you headed back to the keep?"

"Not yet," he said after an unintentionally long pause. "I think I shall get a cup of cocoa and enjoy the snow for a while first. No telling when things will get exciting again."

A VERY PANDA CHRISTMAS, EVERYONE!

Rosemary Jones

"Pa rum pum pum pum." Snowflake loved this song. Shifting the candy cane from the right to the left side of his mouth, he continued to hum "I'm a poor boy too." The music wafted out of the grocery store speakers as he strolled down the now-empty aisles.

Yep, it was a great song. The minute the kid started singing about having no gift to give, the aisles cleared faster than a group of picnicking villains overrun by the Worm Queen's wiggling minions. And if there was one thing that Snowflake hated about the holidays, it was wading through the crowds at his favorite import low-cost bulk buy emporium in the Karlsburg neighborhood.

Pickled bamboo shoots straight from the barrel, lychee nuts bobbing in glowing orangey goodness in big quart bottles, crème de eucalyptus (banned in seven countries and a couple of principalities – how did they get that?) and his absolute favorite holiday treat: sugared grasshopper-stuffed hum bao in rice paper wrapping.

Snowflake sniffed a couple as he dropped the treats into his overflowing shopping cart. "Just like Mom would have made them," the man-panda said to his companion.

"You did not know your mother," Manuel de la Vega muttered. "Ah, *Madre de los Dios*, not that little drummer gringo again!"

Snowflake drew his paw out of his pocket, where he kept Archon's latest remote control. That wonderful gadget overrode the store's music computer random play list and placed his favorite carol in a perpetual loop. "Ain't this place great?" he said with a chomp on the candy cane that shortened the peppermint stick by a full inch.

"Are you done yet?" Manuel might be able to stay on a motorcycle for hours chasing bad guys or chug high octane coffee all night long, but walk the guy down a couple of grocery aisles and he was looking for an exit faster than if one of his ex-girlfriends showed up in town.

"Just need a couple of other items. Then it's back to the kitchen to cook a holiday feast to end all feasts."

Manuel looked doubtful. "Perhaps we should have taken Katherine's offer and gone with the caterers."

"No way," said Snowflake, scooping up the rum-and-coconut-milk frozen treats out of the cold case. After a momentary pause, he also grabbed a dozen champagne popsicles. OK, it was the middle of winter and all the weather reports were promising snow for Christmas. Didn't mean a panda wouldn't want a few cold treats after a big meal.

"You may be dating, or not, the richest woman in Cobalt City," said Snowflake, "but that doesn't mean we abandon the traditional holiday feast created by our own little paws or hands."

"The last time we tried to do this, it did not end well, *amigo*," Manuel began.

"We made the mistake of putting Simon in charge of dessert and attracting Flaming Figgy." Their ashy friend's necromantic field turned his traditional Christmas dessert into a portal for the fiend and the possessed pudding villain had taken nearly a full day to defeat. The resulting wreckage meant Snowflake, Manuel, an apologetic Simon and their guests ended up at Hong Louey's All-Night Dim Sum Diner for Christmas dinner.

"This year, Mister Grey provides the musical entertainment, we do the shopping and the cooking and the party won't be overrun with deadly spirits, other than the kind that people want in their mixed drinks."

"I don't know." Manuel sighed as he stirred a hand through the supplies nearly overflowing the cart. "I am not sure this is what Katherine had in mind when she asked for a Dickensian dinner."

"Wasn't me who took the British babe to the latest holographic adventure remake of *Christmas Carol*."

"That movie received five-star reviews."

"Because they didn't stick to the original. They went off the beaten track."

"The ninja assassins' attack on Marley was very good," Manuel agreed. True, Katherine apparently did not enjoy the movie as much as he expected (although she liked the ninjas), but she had suggested afterward that they all gather for a proper Christmas feast.

"So we're doing the same thing, spicing up tradition with a few unusual appetizers. But the dinner still revolves around one thing and one thing only," said Snowflake as he reached his final destination in the store: the frozen fowl aisle. "The biggest goose that we can find."

"Shouldn't we get a turkey?" asked Manuel.

Snowflake didn't even bother to snort at his friend's ignorance. He'd done his research. Even listened to the original while stripping out the engine of de la Vega's latest bike. A goose it had to be and a goose they would have.

But the bins were gleaming white and lacking in stacked frozen corpses. Where were the birds? A neatly printed sign carried the explanation: "Due to the recent avian pandemic, our regular shipment has been delayed. We are currently working on finding a new supplier. Please leave your name with our butcher."

"The caterer..." started Manuel.

"No need," said Snowflake. "I know Joe."

"Joe?"

"Their meat cleaver. The butcher. He sometimes gets me something special from the back of the truck, if you know what I mean."

"I don't think this is such a good idea."

Snowflake ignored Manuel's protest as he pushed his way through the double doors marked "Employees Only."

"Yo, Joe!" yelled Snowflake. His shout echoed through the stacked up boxes with mysterious scribblings on the side.

"Mr. Snowflake Bear!" came the response from a wizened little old man dressed in a bloodstained apron who popped from behind a crate. "Most happy to see you. Many felicitations of the day."

"Good to see you too!" Snowflake clapped the little man on the shoulder and watched him stagger back a few paces. As a genetic experiment himself, he'd always felt a certain kinship with this little old guy of completely unknowable origins. The wisps of hair ringing his bald head were bright orange but his skin was an odd shade of olive and his slanted eyes sparked green in certain lights. There was also a suggestion of pointedness about the tips of his ears.

"How's it going, Joe?" he asked.

"No so bad, no so good," Joe shrugged.

"Know what you mean," said Snowflake, who didn't have a clue how to interpret Joe's remarks. "Hey, we need a main dish for Christmas dinner: the rarest of all birds; a feathered phenomenon. A really big one!"

"Hmm," said Joe. "I acquire phenomenon last night. No feathers, but very rare. Very big too!"

"Pre-plucked is fine by me. Just quoting Mr. Dickens there."

Snowflake watched Joe disappear into the meat locker and then come staggering back out with a plastic-wrapped carcass.

"Big enough, Mr. Snowflake Bear?" asked Joe, trying to hang onto the large and obviously slippery package.

"Perfect," said Snowflake, lifting the bird from Joe's grasp with one hand and tucking it under his arm. "OK, Manuel, let's check out."

"Shouldn't we get cooking directions or something?"

"No need," repeated Snowflake. "I downloaded all the recipes from The Dickensian Feast Site. Got it all in my netbook back home."

"Do not defrost quickly," said Joe behind them.

"What?" Manuel paused to catch the butcher's advice.

"Thaw slow," said Joe clearly. "No rushing."

"Yeah, yeah," said Snowflake, waving good-bye over his shoulder as he shoved his cart back out the double doors. "We'll take it out the night before. No half-cooked icy bird for us."

The bird was frozen: no doubt whatever about that. Snowflake had forgotten and left it in the freezer until morning. Since then, he'd tried running cold water over it, than warm water, then two teakettles of boiling hot water. He'd even raided Stardust's bathroom at headquarters and borrowed the super-hero's hairdryer. Nothing worked. The old goose was as frozen as an icicle.

Snowflake glanced at the clock. Less than six hours until dinner. According to his calculations and the best advice available from 1-800-COOK-YOUR-GOOSE, he needed at least five hours of cooking time. He'd weighed his prize purchase and it was one big bird, bigger than recommended and probably a little tougher than a younger, smaller goose might be. But Snowflake reminded himself that several guests had superhuman strength and would be easily able to gnaw their way through dinner. And he could carve it so the truly tender bits would go to the merely human types like Manuel or Archon.

But first he had to thaw it.

He poked the plastic-wrapped corpse with one tentative claw. The goose felt like a solid block of ice.

"Crap," muttered Snowflake. He reached into the pocket of his overalls and drew out an emergency candy cane. A bear needed his sweet at a time like this. Snowflake unwrapped the peppermint pick-me-up and stuck it in one side of his mouth, sucking on the stick meditatively.

Obviously, what he needed was a massive source of heat. Something that could thaw this goose in the next thirty minutes so he could get it stuffed and in the oven before everyone arrived. Luckily the usual flurry of holiday emergency calls (lost kittens, grandma attacked by unseen hoofed mammals, fat guy stuck in a chimney, three midnight spirits abusing time travel privileges) had sent everyone flying out of the headquarters early in the day. Some, like the Huntsman, were coming over after spending the morning with family. Others, like Manuel and Archon, would be back as soon as they bolted together a Christmas gift bike for a tearful little boy and his nearly hysterical father.

But even with the technological complexities presented by Christmas toys and instructions in English as written by somebody who didn't speak the language, Snowflake couldn't count on more than a half hour of solitude. Then people would be invading the kitchen and asking awkward questions about why dinner resembled an iceberg.

"The reactor!" Snowflake exclaimed and inhaled his candy cane in one massive crunch of inspiration. Like any well-outfitted super-hero headquarters, the Keep's lab was full of shiny new technology, including Stardust's latest invention: a miniature reactor that powered a warming chamber. The billionaire industrialist had built it to defrost Neanderthal Nick after the Little Green Guy had trapped him in a glacier.

Better yet, Stardust was off in Hawaii, celebrating a sunny Christmas with his family, far away from Cobalt City's December windstorms and icy rains. So he wasn't likely to notice if a bear with a plan invaded his lab.

Snowflake toted the frozen goose to the service elevator. He didn't want to meet any of the returning heroes on his way to or from the reactor room. Nobody ever used the Keep's service elevator except the women who ran the gift shop in the lobby and the plumber who still hadn't figured out why the hot water always ran out halfway through Doctor Shadow's shower. The plumber claimed the pipes were cursed but the mystical Doctor assured everyone that he would spot a curse if it inhabited his bathroom.

Snowflake's theory was that the Doctor always made the mistake of doing his esoteric research as soon as they returned from a fight rather than hopping immediately under the hot water like Katherine or Manuel. By the time that he had finished cross-referencing the lost tablets of Mu with the recently discovered papyrus of the last god-king of Atlantis, the hot water was gone and no spell could summon it back.

The lower levels were quiet and lit with only the solar-charged glow strips that Stardust installed during his energy-saving, have-to-be-the-greenest-super-heroes campaign. In Snowflake's view, being a super-hero was all about having energy to waste. Since he was also at least half highly endangered ursine species, very few people argued with him about ecology.

Snowflake keyed the lockpad that let him into the reactor room. The door slid back with a *whoosh* and the lab beyond sprang into life with the clicking of computers, the blinking of little red lights and the satisfying hum of a miniature nuclear reactor ready to warm his goose to room temperature.

The thawing chamber that Stardust had installed in the center of the lab was a gleaming edifice of stainless steel, gold rivets and a big shiny handle shaped like an old-fashioned ship's wheel. Snowflake grabbed the wheel and spun it to the left. The door didn't budge.

"Righty tighty, lefty loosey," Snowflake muttered. How many times had he told the super genius that simple rule! But Mr. Billionaire Inventor always had to do it his own way. Snowflake spun the wheel to the right and the door to the warming chamber swung out into the room.

Unlike Neanderthal Nick, the goose could be laid flat on the gleaming glass tile floor of the chamber. Snowflake looked down at it. Probably he should peel off the plastic before he hit with the gamma rays. He pulled his penknife out of his pocket, carefully slitting the covering and pulling it off his Christmas goose. Wow, he never realized how ugly a plucked goose was. Nor that they came with the head and the wicked snout intact. And he'd never noticed the big toe claw at the end of the goose's long legs (lot of drumstick there, he thought with satisfaction). Of course, the only time he ever saw real geese, they were swimming around and their legs were under water.

A little frosty water dribbled across the glass surface of the floor, glowing emerald bright in the lights shining up through the tiles. Snowflake fussed with the goose for a moment longer, making sure it was stomach up and rump down in the chamber.

He swung the door closed and, with a sigh, spun the wheel to the left to tighten the seal. Then he walked to the control panel. A pair of giant goggles sat on the top of the panel. There were times when Stardust was reassuringly old school. Snowflake pulled on the goggles, settling them on his nose. The protective lens made the whole room look slightly green around the edges.

The big black temperature dial had three settings: warm, hot and extreme. Snowflake glanced at the clock. Less than twenty minutes until he needed to pop the goose in the oven. He shoved the dial to extreme, pulled the big silver on-off lever to the on position and flipped open the glass cover on the glowing red button with the yellow warning label. He always loved this

40

moment and nobody ever let him do this as much as he liked. He slammed his paw down on the button.

Sirens wailed a warning, lights flashed in a tidal wave of cascading blinks around the room and the miniature nuclear reactor slipped into a higher key of hum.

The thawing chamber vibrated slightly in the middle of the room. The needle on the center dial of the control panel began to tick up from zero to 100 percent radiation. Two smaller dials on the side of the panel had wildly oscillating needles spinning between yellow, green and red sections. Snowflake ignored those.

An intercom on the control panel hissed. It was a general hail coming from the living quarters above.

"Merry Christmas," Wild Kat's voice warbled through the intercom. "We're coming down the chimney, ho, ho, ho!" Then the slight hissing sound that you always got when using the outside intercom on the rooftop landing pad. Then Snowflake could hear Wild Kat speaking to someone else outside. "No answer. I wonder where they are."

The sonorous tones of Doctor Shadow sounded through the connection: "Most likely they are busy with the preparation of the meal."

"Yes, yes," said Manuel's probable ladylove. "Thank you for helping me with these packages and flying me here. It was just a lot to load in the cab and I gave the staff the day off. If you can fetch that big bag and I'll take this one..."

Snowflake let out a frustrated growl. The dial's needle was still way off its final mark and it would have to tick back down to zero radiation before he could unlock the chamber door.

Time for diversionary tactics. He could scoot back up to the kitchen, chuck some hum bao in the microwave for appetizers and get Wild Kat and the good Doctor working on some project in the dining room. Table decoration. The British heiress and society queen of Cobalt City would want to rearrange the table settings and maybe even set the Doctor to folding the napkins into swan shapes, something the nimble-fingered ancient Egyptian did with definitive panache.

Snowflake shoved the goggles up on his forehead and sprinted for the service elevator, leaving the door to the lab open behind him.

Up in the kitchen, he threw frozen Chinese appetizers in the microwave, chucked the champagne bottles through the air to land with a satisfying ring in the ice buckets, stirred the applesauce bubbling on the stove, mashed a few potatoes in passing and made sure that his stuffing was hidden in the oven. It wouldn't dry out totally in the few minutes that he needed before he could return to the lower levels and grab the thawed goose. Besides, the smell of sage, onion and cornbread warming in the oven might mask the lack of bird.

He'd barely had time to wrap Manuel's "Kiss the Cook" apron around his middle before Wild Kat poked her head through the kitchen door.

"How is the dinner coming?"

"Fine."

"Are we the first ones here? I thought you might appreciate some assistance."

"Sure!" Snowflake shifted so he was between Wild Kat and Doctor Shadow and the rest of the kitchen. The advantage of being a generously proportioned man-panda was that they couldn't see around him. "The others are out on calls."

"Even Manuel?" Wild Kat's face fell.

"Yeah, but he should be back soon. It was an emergency bike assembly, but he took Archon with him."

Snowflake kept advancing on his guests, essentially backing them into the dining room. The gleaming silver and china was piled on the table, but no places had been set.

"Maybe you guys could help me with this. Manuel was going to do it when he got back…"

"Of course," said Wild Kat, heading toward the table with a gleam in her eye. "Let's see, we have six coming: you, me, Archon, Simon, Manuel and the Doctor."

"Velvet, the Huntsman and Gallows called. They caught the Bad Elf and can be here for dinner. The Worm Queen has other plans. Invited to some University party."

"Nine, then. We are going to need the extension for the table. Where did we put it after that last big intertemporal congress of heroes?"

"Storage closet. Upstairs. I think," said Snowflake. He didn't know but looking for the extra leaves for the table would keep her busy.

"And me?" A faint smile creased Doctor Shadow's face. "Swan napkins, I presume."

"That would be great, Doc."

"I have a new method for this year," said the master of mystery. He settled into a chair at the head of the table and fixed his glowing gaze upon the pile of snowy napkins. The top one quivered and slowly floated toward the ceiling, twisting itself into a swan shape and then gliding in gentle spirals to its proper place on the table.

"Great. Great," Snowflake backed through the door into the kitchen and then turned and sprinted toward the service elevator.

At the lobby level, the service elevator came to a stop and the doors slid open to reveal a startled Manuel.

"What are you doing here?" he and Snowflake said simultaneously.

"Archon wanted to sneak some packages under the tree," said Manuel. "And he did not want me to know his hiding place in the Keep. Like I would reveal his secret gift stash! But what are you doing? How is the dinner cooking?"

"Fine," Snowflake reached for the "door close" button. "Just need to get something from the basement."

Manuel's eyes narrowed with the suspicion that only an old friend could direct at a furry brother trying to look innocent. "Why are you wearing goggles?"

"Uh," Snowflake reached up to drag the revelatory headgear off and stuffed it into a pocket. He shrugged. "Eye protection is important when cooking?"

Manuel sprang through the elevator doors before they closed. "What something? Where?"

Snowflake gave up on his attempt at deception. He could lie to Manuel (and did when necessary), but right now, the truth would get him an assistant cook with a good reason to keep his mouth shut. Manuel had made many promises to Wild Kat, not the least of which was that the dinner would be served on time and without incident this Christmas.

"I had some problems with the goose."

"What problems?"

"The goose was a little cold this morning."

"*Güey,*" Manuel sighed.

"*Dude,*" Snowflake drawled back. "I fixed it. We just fetch the bird, shuttle it back to the kitchen, stuff some breadcrumbs and oysters up its butt and pop it into the oven."

The elevator doors slid open on the lower level. Snowflake wrinkled his nose at the smell of burnt plastic and seared flesh wafting down the corridor. Maybe the extreme setting had been a bit much.

He started toward the lab, noting that the door appeared to be hanging halfway off its hinges.

A shriek of rage exploded down the hallway, a high-pitched scream of aggravation.

"*Hijole!*" Manuel froze behind him in the corridor.

Snowflake skidded to stop. His sensitive panda ears picked up the screech of long claws against linoleum.

"Manuel," he said, backing away from the broken door to the lab. Past the ruined door, he saw a shadow of definitely dinosaurian shape slide across the wall. "Do you have any weapons?"

"Weapons? I have a screwdriver. The kid's father handed it to me and I forgot to give it back."

Snowflake stuck out a paw. "Give! And then run for the elevator."

Another scream erupted from the lab.

"What is in there?" Manuel passed him the screwdriver but stayed where he was.

"Christmas dinner. I think it is mad."

A velociraptor leaped into the hall. Slightly bigger than a well-stuffed turkey, it lunged at Snowflake with another shriek. It sprang high, going for his throat with its toe spur. Snowflake ducked and rolled, jabbing upward with the screwdriver as the irradiated and irritated dinosaur sailed overhead. He missed.

With a growl, Snowflake surged upward, trying to grapple his too lively main dish to the ground. The slippery dinosaur twisted out of his grip. It snapped at Snowflake's belly but only ended up with a mouthful of "Kiss Me" apron. It pulled away, shredding the apron. Snowflake backhanded it with a mighty thump to the thorax. Out of the corner of his eye, he could see Manuel circling, trying to get in position for his own attack.

Snowflake lunged and weaved, attempting to keep the velociraptor focused on him rather than the man sneaking up behind it. The angry little dinosaur kept snapping and slashing at him. Apparently it wanted nothing more than a bite of bear for its first meal after thawing out.

"Anytime now," Snowflake said as he feinted to the left and bobbed to the right. The toe spur went slashing way, way too close to sensitive parts of his anatomy. He was glad he had worn the super-sized brass belt buckle with the rampaging reindeer. The dinosaur's claw rang on his buckle like a clapper of a bell and Snowflake rolled out of the way, hoping Manuel could get a clear shot at the creature.

Manuel spun on his heel, kicking straight out with one leg like a Kung Fu Scrooge confronted by a dozen ninjas of Christmas past. He caught the angry velociraptor directly on the tip of its snout. The enraged dinosaur screamed and twisted in mid-air. It hit the tiles and skidded past Manuel toward the service elevator doors.

The velociraptor collided against the metal elevator doors with the crash of dinosaur meets steel. It stumbled to its feet, shaking its head.

Taking advantage of the dinosaur's momentary confusion, Snowflake threw the screwdriver at it like a javelin. The tool whistled through the air. Manuel bent backwards as it flew past his nose. The screwdriver also flew past the velociraptor's head to hit the elevator call button. A perfect bull's-eye that opened the elevator doors. The dinosaur rolled one groggy eye at the panting man-panda and his stunned Mexican friend. It stumbled backward into the elevator. The doors slammed shut and it was gone.

Snowflake looked at Manuel. His friend looked back at him.

"Maybe it will be trapped in there?" Snowflake didn't have much hope. With the way that the day had been going, the doors were sure to open in the upper levels, releasing the furious velociraptor in the middle of a crowd expecting to eat a stuffed goose rather than be eaten by a defrosted dinosaur.

With a shake of his head, Manuel sprinted down the hallway toward the front elevators. Snowflake pounded after him.

Manuel hit the button. It lit up. He jiggled in place, making Snowflake twitch sympathetically.

"It might go to the roof," Snowflake said.

"Did the Flaming Figgy appear on the roof?"

Manuel had a point. Disaster, when it struck, tended to show up in the middle of the dinner table.

With a ping, the elevator doors slid open. Snowflake hit the button for the second floor and the dining room.

Upstairs they heard the wails of despair before they saw the destruction.

"My centerpiece!" yowled Wild Kat. "The presents!"

"My swan napkins," moaned Doctor Shadow.

Only Archon sounded calm as the velociraptor sprang to the center of the dining room table to wreak carnage on Wild Kat's carefully constructed centerpiece of gifts, artfully placed fresh fruit and other special tidbits in crystal dishes.

"See, I told you that the movies got their size all wrong," Archon said. He waved a hand at Snowflake and Manuel to acknowledge their arrival but kept his eyes fixed on his computer screen as he punched through the codes, obviously searching for more information on the reptilian invader of their dining room. "Yes, all the fossil evidence clearly shows that this breed of dromaeosaurid never grew larger than a turkey,"

"Or a goose," muttered Snowflake, circling right around the table as the velociraptor shredded a Satsuma orange out of its red tissue wrapping. The fowl-sized dinosaur seemed less interested in the crowd surrounding the table than the food before it. The velociraptor nosed its way through a box of foil-wrapped chocolates and macadamia nuts shipped from Hawaii, a gift from Stardust and family.

"So how do we kill it?" asked Manuel.

"Kill it?" said Archon. "We cannot kill it. This is an endangered species. There's only one known breeding pair in North America. They and their offspring were stolen more than a month ago."

46

"Stolen?" asked Snowflake innocently. Behind him, Manuel sighed noisily but he didn't squeal about Joe. Before him, the velociraptor discovered the bowl of walnuts and carefully cracked each nut with one bite, littering the tabletop with shells.

"A whole zoo of exotics was heisted by some unscrupulous gourmands," Archon explained, as he loved to do. "They planned to sell them to various restaurants for holiday menus. There's people who will pay enormous sums to eat unusual or endangered animals for Christmas, like flying reindeer burgers."

"Yech," said Wild Kat.

"Luckily, most of the zoo stock were recovered when somebody tipped the police about seeing a refrigeration warehouse filled with wooly mammoth." Archon tapped his computer to do a quick check of the police reports. "Yes, all the prehistoric creatures were recovered except one Tyrannosaurus egg and an adolescent male velociraptor."

The purloined dinosaur overturned the now-empty nut bowl with a disappointed screech and then dived for the tray of caviar, exotic cheeses, crackers and dried fruit. Judging from Wild Kat's howl of pure rage, that was one of her contributions to the party. The girl did like her expensive hors d'oeuvres.

Ignoring Manuel's shout of protest, Wild Kat cart wheeled across the table, snatching the caviar dish from under the velociraptor's nose and vaulted to safety, flipping in midair to land on her feet like her feline namesake.

"That's two hundred dollars an ounce!" she said to Manuel, cradling the crystal dish of caviar close to her curvaceous chest. "I'm not letting some reptile swallow it."

"So what do we do with it?" said Snowflake. "Call animal control?"

"Most likely they are enjoying their holiday at home. It would be better to restrain it ourselves," said Archon. "Now, let me see what would be the best…"

But Doctor Shadow intervened. "That is enough!" he thundered at the velociraptor as it pounced again upon one of his artfully constructed swan napkins, shaking out its snowy folds. He levitated out of his chair, holding his hands level with his hips and palms out as he began to chant a spell that had been first used in the court of Ramses the Great.

47

As Doctor Shadow's voice rose and fell, reciting the ancient Egyptian verses, the remaining swan napkins took flight, twisting like a linen tornado toward the dinosaur. Deprived of its cloth prey, the velociraptor began one of its toe slashing leaps toward the Doctor. But the swan napkins surrounded it, spinning faster and faster as each napkin unraveled into a long strip, binding the velociraptor from tail tip to snout.

It wobbled for a moment in place and then fell off the table with a crash.

"Wow," said Wild Kat, looking at the linen-wrapped dinosaur. "You mummified it."

"Only temporarily," said Doctor Shadow, floating gently back to the floor. "No harm has come to it and the spell can be easily reversed to release it once it has been transported back to its proper home."

"Good work," said Archon. "I will alert the zoo officials that we will be bringing back their lost dinosaur tomorrow. I assume it is safe to leave it like this for Christmas?"

Doctor Shadow nodded and waved one hand. The newly mummified dinosaur slid to the far side of the room, gliding to a halt under the Christmas tree. At the lift of the Doctor's eyebrow, a large red bow and glittery gift tag appeared around the velociraptor's neck. "It seems more festive that way," the mystic of the ages said. "Tomorrow I will send it back to the zoo."

"But what are we doing about dinner?" hissed Manuel to Snowflake as Wild Kat dipped an absent-minded finger into her bowl of caviar.

Snowflake reached into his pocket and pulled out his cell phone. "Just call me a boy scout. I'm prepared for an emergency," he said, hitting the speed dial for Hong Louey's All Night Dim Sum Diner. "Louey? Snowflake here. Can we get those Peking ducks to go? And some extra Szechuan noodles? Sixty minutes? Make it thirty and Manuel will double your tip."

Hours later, surrounded by the wreckage of a good meal eaten with good friends, Snowflake propped his elbows on the table and gazed a little drunkenly at the gathering. The latecomers, Simon, Velvet, the Huntsman and Gallows were all standing around the temporarily mummified dinosaur and asking for details again on how it had eaten all of the Christmas chocolate before they had arrived. Manuel had one arm wrapped around Wild Kat's shoulders, threatening her playfully with a sprig of mistletoe.

Outside the windows, the snow began to fall, sparkling briefly in the reflected light from the room before disappearing into the darkness below.

"Next year, we can try for a goose again," Snowflake said to Doctor Shadow.

"Or maybe we should call a caterer," the sage one suggested.

"I think we should do a turkey," said Wild Kat, batting away the mistletoe. "Like in *Christmas Carol*."

"It was a goose, stuffed goose," said Snowflake. "I listened to the audiobook."

"Cratchit's family had this puny goose," said Wild Kat. "But Scrooge sent the boy out for a turkey, the biggest one in the butcher shop window. I don't know why I loved that book so, but I used to read it every year. My father had the most beautiful leather-bound edition with these lovely black-and-white drawings of Scrooge, Bob Cratchit and Tiny Tim."

"My father always read that story out loud on Christmas Eve," said Simon. The man of ash drifted back to the table. "Odd. I remember the ghosts used to frighten me terribly. Especially the ghost of Christmas Yet To Come, the one that showed Scrooge his own grave."

"So, a turkey," said Snowflake. "Guess I wasn't listening that closely."

"It's the thought that counts," said Manuel. "You did, in the end, provide us with a great Christmas dinner."

"Hear, hear," said Simon and the others joined him in a round of applause for Snowflake's feast.

"Well, I might have been mistaken about the goose," said Snowflake with a shrug and no further elaboration about what exactly had been wrong with his fowl choice. "But I have the right toast for tonight and all you Dickens fans will appreciate it."

"What?"

Snowflake rose to his feet and raised his glass to the gathered super-heroes of Cobalt City. The man-panda grinned at them. As he recited the ancient benediction, they all began to laugh and join in: "God Bless Us, Every One!"

SILENT KNIGHTS: HOLIDAY PARTY

Nathan Crowder

It was the social event of the season for Cobalt City: the Grand Holiday Gala. Since 1959, the Gandry family had hosted, and this year the Gandry patriarch—ruthlessly wealthy Titus Gandry—had assembled a guest list of the brightest shining stars on the scene. Guests included two movie stars, a hip-hop producer, the head of a major Russian corporation, Senator Finlay who was recently made head of the Energy and Natural Resources Committee, and British-born heiress Katherine Wilde.

Katherine should have been able to enjoy the party, but fate had other plans. Croatian assassin Victor Cross had entered the city two days ago, sending up red flags all over New England. Katherine's lover and fellow vigilante, Manuel de la Vega, had taken over tracking him as soon as the feared killer stepped off the airplane. In his alter ego of Gato Loco, he and Cross had bumped heads four times - once in Cobalt City, once in New Orleans, and twice in Mexico City. Four encounters, and out of those, Cross had killed his target three times. Neither Manuel nor Katherine wanted a fourth on their watch.

With her leather costume modified to be worn beneath the expensive, red Vera Wang dress, Wild Kat was on her third circuit through the decked-out home in the gated suburbs. She and Manuel had determined Senator Finlay to be the most likely target, and keeping between him and an unseen assassin was not the kind of assignment she cared for. Katherine was a woman of action – her alter ego Wild Kat even more so. Waiting for a bullet out of the darkness was not her style.

When the lights went out, she was so relieved to be in action that she shifted into her feline form without a second thought for the red silk gown falling around her feet in ribbons. Her ears

50

shifted higher on her head and her brow became more pronounced while sinews became more corded and rippled beneath her skin with each movement. Claws like obsidian blades sprouted from her hands and feet, and flesh-rending incisors extended within her mouth. Her senses, her strength, her reflexes, all increased exponentially. Slit-like pupils opened wide and round, scanning the room for Senator Finlay.

The steady red dot from the sniper's rifle told her where to find the unaware politician. With his secret service detail still shouting in their radios, trying to determine if there was a threat, Wild Kat cleared the buffet table in an easy hop, and dropped the target into cover. Heightened hearing picked up the POP POP TINKLE of two bullets putting one hole through the panes of the bay window at the end of the room. She had maneuvered her body enough to be in the path of the deadly bullets, but felt nothing. She had acted in time, and Senator Finlay was safe.

"North lawn," she growled into her communicator to Gato Loco. She turned her attention to the senator, overlooking the way he was unable to avoid staring at the auburn hair tumbling down into her leather-enhanced cleavage. "And you, senator, stay put. Your security detail will handle it from here."

"He's on the move," Gato Loco replied. "I'm on him, but I think he ditched something near the squirrel hedge."

Not satisfied to leave the collar to Gato Loco, she sprang to her feet in the still-darkened room and bounded towards the sniper's nest. Four acrobatic leaps and a tray of spilled drinks later, Wild Kat burst through the compromised window onto the snow-dusted north lawn of the Gandry estate. She could already see the disappearing taillights of Gato Loco's sleek, black motorcycle.

Wild Kat had clocked her top land speed at 58 miles per hour. There was no way she could catch up with the two men on cycles. Instead she sighted on the topiary trimmed to resemble a giant squirrel, finding the discarded black nylon kit bag within seconds. It didn't take her long to determine there was no rifle within, merely a thick file – the profile on the target, who, much to her surprise, had not been the senator.

After flipping through three pages of the folder, she understood why someone wanted this person dead. She touched base with the central switchboard via communicator before doubling back to the house. A black Mercedes was pulled up to the front door by the time she got there. The scent of vodka, cigar, and stale sweat mingled with blood, telling her that Cross had wounded the target – perhaps intentionally. The Russian limped towards the car with his two guards, his footsteps scarlet in the snow. Yes, definitely wounded.

The guards saw Wild Kat coming and drew their pistols. She had disarmed the first before he could bring the barrel around, and the second guard fired wildly into the ground. A swipe of her claws and that pistol spun off into the snow. "Vladimir Greshenko," she growled, "the police are on their way to take you in to custody. They are coming with an ambulance to look to your injuries as well."

"You have nothing," the Russian sneered. His guards did nothing, knowing when they were beaten.

"Wrong. I have an open line to the Protectorate's switchboard and the Cobalt City Police. Cobalt's boys in blue will be most interested to talk to you about a container full of women at the harbor that they will be discovering any minute," she said. "I have it on good authority that one of the women has a father with deep pockets. He hired someone to find the girl and get vengeance. He didn't want you dead. He wanted you to suffer a long time for your crimes."

The sounds of police sirens lanced the icy winter air. No guards, a wounded leg, and Wild Kat breathing down his neck – Greshenko knew when he was beaten. His shoulders sagged. "What witchcraft is this? How do you know these things?"

"Someone left a file for me under a tree," she answered, a ghost of a smile upon her lips, "It couldn't have been more welcome if he had put a bow on it. It's just what I wanted for the holidays."

NUTCRACKER

Angel Leigh McCoy

Nutcracker bent over the tombstone. The only name on it was: Ballerina. She had maintained her anonymity to the very end. Even Nutcracker didn't know her real name, but that didn't matter to him. He had loved the tiny dancer more than anything in the world.

Ballerina had put more than one serial killer into oblivion with a chassé, grand battement and plié combination. She liked to say she had killer attitude. As partners against crime, she and Nutcracker had taken down some of Cobalt City's worst masterminds.

Beneath her name was a single date, her deathday. It read, "June 16, 2007."

Nutcracker had never managed to get the image of her body—broken and bleeding, sprawled on the street—out of his mind. She had looked like an angel fallen from Heaven, or a fairytale swan caught in the wrong reality. The rain, the dirt and the bloodstain had swallowed her up, overcoming the pure white of her leotard and flattening her tutu. Her hair had come loose from her bun and was flowing in the stream along the gutter, as if she herself were being flushed away. Nutcracker carried the sight with him ever since.

The wind and sky held the promise of snow. Lafayette Cemetery was a watercolor in shades of gray, with rows of headstones commemorating the deaths of Cobalt City's greatest heroes. The cold seeped into Nutcracker's joints and made his eyes blurry with wind-whipped moisture.

DNA Man approached slowly, making as much noise as possible. Before he was within striking distance, he said, "Merry Christmas, Nut."

53

Nutcracker didn't even look up. He didn't have to. "I fucking hate Christmas."

"How can you hate Christmas? What's there to hate?"

"Don't get me started," Nutcracker said. "I hate the fucking baubles and the boozers. I hate the music. Insipid or boring—there's no in between. I hate the shoppers. I hate the stupid fuckers who wear reindeer horns, sequined elf sweaters and Santa hats. I hate that fat old bastard in the red suit who never stops smiling, not even when you smear dog shit in his face. Most of all, I hate kids, especially that little brat who turned me in for defiling *Santa Claus*. For Christ's sake. If people would quit lying to their offspring, maybe we'd have fewer assholes in the world."

DNA Man wrapped his arms around himself and shifted from foot to foot. "Aren't you a fucking bundle of joy, mate."

"What are you doing here, Dee?" Nutcracker finally raised his eyes and took in the haggard, hunched appearance of his once-friend. He noted the way the tweed trousers no longer fit him properly and how the sleeves on his overcoat hung too far down his hands. He didn't need to count the shadows on Dee's face to know that they had multiplied since the last time. "You looking for me or just out for an anonymous graveyard B.J.?"

Dee sneered. "You offering, or just being an asshole?"

"Hey, I ain't the one who got arrested for public perversion."

"Asshole," said Dee. "Whatever."

"It's that attitude that got you positive, idiot." Nutcracker couldn't stop himself. He had known the man who had cheated on and then infected Dee. They'd had years of dinner parties, vacations and even Christmases together, back before Ballerina had died, back when Dee had still been his best friend, back when things like carolers and Santas with bells hadn't made him want to change the color of his hat from white to black. Back before life itself had betrayed him.

Dee pulled his collar tighter around his chicken neck. "That and the fact that I'm a stupid, cock-sucking queer who trusted the wrong guy." He sounded exhausted. "I'm not gonna have this same conversation again. I know how you feel and besides, I'm here for a reason. Nasty sent me."

"I figured." Nutcracker bent and placed the single, red rose beside Ballerina's tombstone.

Dee sighed, "Aren't you going to ask what she wants?"

"What's she want?"

Dee shrugged. "Well, if you're not interested, then I'll just go back and tell her I couldn't find you."

Nutcracker stood slowly, smoothing his creased, blue trousers as he did. He faced Dee. "Don't be a twinkle-toes. You're not my bitch. Just tell me what she wants."

"She's got a job for us."

"Okay," said Nutcracker, stuffing his hands deep into the pockets of his red long-coat. "Now tell me something I hadn't already guessed." He turned on his heel and headed toward the parking lot.

With a quick step or two, Dee fell into stride with Nutcracker. He had to shuffle more quickly to keep up with Nutcracker's long legs. He said, "It's about the kid."

"What about the kid?"

"Mouse is back."

Nutcracker halted in place. "When?"

Dee stopped a moment later and turned. "Not sure. He's been spotted. That's all I know. Nasty's bringing everyone in. She needs us to pick up the package and meet at the clubhouse."

"Why didn't you say so? Key-rist!" Nutcracker clacked his teeth together and double-timed it to his car.

On any other day, on any other mission, Nutcracker would have waited in the car while Dee went in to retrieve the package. On this day, on this mission, his nerves jangled him right out onto the sidewalk in front of the building. He kept his back to the spot where Ballerina had died, but it climbed up his spine like a kitten. Pacing didn't help either, because at a certain point he had to do an about-face and there it would be: the mailbox, the fire hydrant and the gutter.

Just when he felt he couldn't stand it anymore, just when the memories had reached a screaming fever-pitch in his brain, just when he was thinking it might be easier after all if he went inside to those familiar rooms, Dee emerged from the building.

Mary skipped along beside him. "Nut!" she cried and ran straight to him. He caught her in his arms and lifted her in a big, twirling hug fueled by the state of his nerves.

Mary squealed and wrapped her arms and legs around him. She wore a red and green pants outfit with shiny patent-leather shoes. Her white-blond hair was pulled into a long braid. She was the most darling child imaginable. As beautiful as any china doll, she had pale skin, blue eyes and angel hair. She had begun reading at three. By five, she had been able to recite the alphabet in both directions and knew her multiplication tables up through twelvesies. At six, she had spontaneously begun speaking Spanish to the cleaning lady. At seven, she was deconstructing Proust.

No sooner had the hugging begun than it had to end. Nutcracker put the girl back on her feet and scanned the area. "We got to go, Mary. Get in the car."

Mary had a special place in the super-heroes' hearts. She was Ballerina's daughter.

"I'm sorry, people. I know it's Christmas Eve." Nasty Girl stood at the front of the war room, hands on hips, legs spread and rooted. In all respects, she looked like a bag lady who'd been living on the streets for a decade, except one: she had a pretty face. The fineness of her features amidst all that filth made her look like a kid in a Halloween costume.

Nasty looked from one to the other of the heroes gathered there: Miss Creant, The X, DNA Man and Nutcracker. The five of them made up the Nasty Brigade. They were a motley bunch built from the dregs of the local super-hero population. None of the respectable groups—like the Protectorate or the Mysterious Five—wanted them, for various reasons. Nasty Girl's powers came from the grime and grit of the city streets. On a good day— when she didn't reek of vomit, piss, or dog shit—she smelled like car exhaust.

Miss Creant had a minor problem with kleptomania that kept her out of the more respectable super-hero groups. DNA Man came with a communicable disease and that made him a pariah in every circle, even non-super-hero ones. The X was just unbelievably strange and Nutcracker was, well, a flaming asshole.

Despite all their faults and not counting the days when they were dangerously close to becoming super-villains, the members of the Nasty Brigade did good. They helped old ladies cross streets, found lost pets and protected children.

"Cut to the chase, Nasty," said Nutcracker. "What's going on?"

Nasty eyed Nutcracker and everyone could tell she was holding back a sharp comment. Instead, she said, "Mouse is in Cobalt City."

Sighs and head-shaking abounded. Mouse had once been a member of the Nasty Brigade. He had the ability to reduce himself—and anything or anyone he was touching—to the size of a mouse or to grow as large as a house. Most often, he chose the small size for easier get-aways.

More than once, Mouse had crossed over to the evil side of the street. Nasty had reprimanded him repeatedly before finally showing him the door. If it hadn't been for Ballerina, Mouse would have been out on his ear much sooner, but Ballerina had stood up for him. She and Mouse had been lovers—a fact that Nutcracker still found difficult to chew.

Nutcracker said, "How long's he been in the city?"

"We're not sure," Nasty replied. "He's being particularly stealthy this time."

Miss Creant asked, "Is Mary in the safehouse?"

Nasty nodded. "I had Dee and Nut move her here as soon as I heard Mouse was in town."

"Surely," said Nut, "you don't think he'll try to snatch her again—not after the smackdown we gave him last time he tried."

Nasty's expression was grim. "That's exactly what I think. We all know Mouse. He's stubborn and single-minded. Once he gets something stuck in his head, nothing can get it out. He's here for Mary, again."

The X raised a black-gloved hand.

Everyone turned to look at him, silent. The X hardly ever spoke and when he did, it was always poignant. He wore a black silk cape with a cowl that covered his head. Dark, beetle eyes gleamed in his negroid face.

Nasty nodded for him to speak.

The X said, "He IS the child's father."

Everyone nodded and waited, but that was all the X had to say.

Finally, Nasty replied. She said, "It doesn't matter. He lost his parental rights the night he killed Ballerina."

Nutcracker paced outside Mary's room. He could hear her in there, singing "Ave Maria" to herself. She had a dulcet voice.

Dee came down the hall. "Hey. Looks like it's you and me, pal. Just like ol' times."

"Trust me," said Nutcracker. "This is nothing like *ol' times*." He continued pacing. "I should be out there, looking for him."

"No, you shouldn't. The most likely place for him to show up is here. Especially tonight." Dee leaned against the wall. "You know how he is. Every year at this time, he gets nostalgic. Maybe he has a few too many drinks. Maybe he gets overwhelmed by a massive mope. Whatever the case, he ends up getting into trouble."

A burst of little-girl laughter came from inside Mary's room.

Dee chuckled. "She sure can entertain herself."

"Do it again!" Mary clapped. "Do it again!"

Nutcracker and Dee locked eyes and froze. A second later, they both launched themselves into action. Nutcracker got to the door first and flung it open.

Mary was sitting on the safe house bed. She was laughing and clapping as a man shifted in size from tiny to normal in front of her.

"Mouse," said Nutcracker, "you son of a bitch. I'm gonna go nemesis on your ass." He threw himself at the other man as if to tackle him. He knew better. It was a lesson he'd learned more than once and apparently needed to learn again.

Mouse dropped back down to mouse size and skittered away.

Nutcracker grabbed empty air and landed hard against the dresser beyond where Mouse had been standing. "Mother-fucker!"

Dee said, "Nut. There's a kid here."

"Well, get her out of here." Nutcracker got to his feet.

A third voice spoke up, an unexpected one. "What are you doing?" it demanded to know. Seven-year-old Mary had moved to stand on the bed, her arms crossed tightly on her chest in a stance that reminded Nutcracker painfully of Ballerina. She was glaring at him.

"I'm...." Nutcracker didn't have time to say more. Out of the corner of his eye, he saw Mouse run between the dresser and the chair. "Aha!" he said. "I've got you now." He picked up the chair and threw it across the room, revealing a shocked Mouse, a tiny Mouse, huddling there. As quick as a wink, Nutcracker made a grab for him.

A little-girl shriek filled the air. It split Nutcracker's head in two, or at least, felt like it. His hands flew to cover his ears.

Everyone in the room, including Mouse, turned to stare at Mary. No one moved.

"Leave him alone! He's mine!"

"He's a criminal, honey," Dee said. "We have to take him to jail."

"No!" Mary's lips scrunched tightly. "He's mine." She jumped off the bed and walked to the corner where Mouse cowered. She placed herself between him and Nutcracker. Crossing her arms on her chest, she put on her stubborn face.

"Now look, kid," said Nutcracker. "This is grown-up stuff. I know you like the little guy, but he won't always be little. He'll get big and then what will you do?"

"I don't care. He's mine."

Nutcracker cast a frustrated glance at Dee, who shrugged in response.

A sudden, loud thud made both men hunch and look around wildly.

"What the fuck?" came a small, squeaky voice. While the others were distracted, Mouse had begun to slip sideways, into the shadows under the armoire. He hadn't gotten far.

"Well, I'll be goddammed," said Nutcracker. He looked at Mary. "Did you do that?"

She smiled sweetly and nodded. "I used a pressure panel to trigger it."

"Get me out of here!" squeaked Mouse. He stared out through the iron bars of the cage. It had dropped down onto him from above when he ran toward the armoire. As they watched, he squinched up his face and grew big enough to fill the cage, but no

59

bigger. He looked uncomfortable with flabby bits pooching out through the bars.

"It's iron," said Mary. "The molecular make-up of iron is unique in that it doesn't conduct transmutative energies."

Dee stepped forward and bent to see Mouse better. "You mean he can't get any bigger than the cage?"

Mary squatted by the cage. "Yup."

Dee was the first to laugh, his oboe tones free and easy. He was joined by Mary's airy, flute-like giggles. Eventually, even Nutcracker had to join them. His laughter rumbled, deep and long like the sound of a tuba. Mouse's squeaking complaints were the piccolo.

The cookies and milk arrived soon and the whole team came to laugh at Mouse in his cage. They patted Mary on the back for her ingenuity.

"Whatever gave you the idea?" asked Nasty Girl.

Mary shrugged. "I dunno. I wanted a gerbil, but a mouse will do."

"And you did this all by yourself?" asked Miss Creant as she slipped a few cookies into her pocket.

"Yeah," said Mary.

"Where'd you get the cage?" asked Dee.

"I made it."

Nasty slid down the wall, leaving a brownish yellow stain, and sat with her back against it. "You made it?"

"Sure." Mary shrugged. "It was easy. I found some old fireplace tools and I just bent them to make the cage."

"You bent them? How?"

A sly smile spread across Mary's face. She replied, "With my teeth."

Surprised looks appeared on some faces, confused looks on others.

The X nodded sagely and said, "Like father, like daughter."

All eyes turned to Mouse.

"But," said Nutcracker. "Mouse doesn't have super biting power. He just changes size."

All eyes turned to Nutcracker.

60

"I suspected as much," said Dee.

"Suspected what?" asked Nutcracker, looking back at everyone.

Nasty Girl chuckled. "She obviously didn't get her brains from you, too."

Nutcracker's mouth dropped open and he shot his gaze to Mary. She was looking up at him, her Ballerina eyes bright, her grin broad and toothy. Of course, *she* had already figured it out.

Dee moved to stand beside Nutcracker and put his arm around the other man's broad shoulders. He said, "Merry Christmas, Nut. Looks like you got the best present of all."

Nutcracker didn't reply for a moment. He couldn't. He had a lump in his throat the size of the moon. When he did speak, he said, "Well, merry fucking Christmas," and he grinned a grin as broad and toothy as Mary's.

Everyone laughed.

Mary pirouetted and said, "I'm going to dance for you now. Okay?"

"Yes, please," said Nutcracker.

Mouse sat down in the corner of his cage and squeaked, "I hate you all."

GHOST OF CHRISTMAS PAST

Jeremy Zimmerman

"Are you sure about this, boss?" Snowflake asked over the radio. The question had come out of the blue, the uplifted panda's voice on the earpiece jolting Gato Loco out of his reverie.

The leather-clad super-hero had parked his bike, Shadow, a few blocks away and approached the crumbling old mansion on foot. The snow was coming down hard, leaving Gato Loco wishing he'd asked the Tesla Twins to put some heating into the complex leather suit. His bike seemed very far away and he wasn't certain he could still feel his one functional testicle.

Snowflake was supposed to be parked in his truck nearby, as backup. Gato Loco wasn't sure what Snowflake would do if something really bad happened. At the very least, someone could call and let people know that it was time for a funeral.

"No," replied Gato Loco.

"We can back out any time you want," Snowflake suggested. "There's a great little Chinese place I passed on the way in. It's Christmas Eve, but they should still be open."

"This was a one-time invitation," Gato Loco answered. "I'm too curious to let it just slide."

"You know what they say about curiosity, boss…"

A few days prior, detective Manuel de la Vega had received an anonymous package containing a map. At a glance, it appeared to lead to a Cobalt City mansion in the decaying Karlsburg neighborhood, and contained an invitation to receive his Christmas present. It caught Manuel's attention because it specifically linked him with his cowled alter-ego, Gato Loco. It sounded like a trap, but he couldn't ignore it either as a detective or a super-hero vigilante.

Research had dug up ownership by a family named "Carlton." It had been in the family since the 19th century, but no one had lived in it for at least twenty years. The current owner and last surviving member of the Carlton clan, Julie Carlton, was a recluse who spent most of her time in Manhattan. She was a noted philanthropist that no one ever saw. ("It's a perfect formula for a super-villain," Snowflake had insisted.) Rumor claimed the mansion was haunted and urban legends of people meeting their doom in this building dotted the Internet.

The wrought iron gates that barred the driveway were left hanging open, an ominous invitation for the vigilante. Sticking to the shadows cast by the few streetlights working nearby, Gato Loco slunk closer to the building. As he skirted around the overgrown shrubbery, his police training and night vision filters showed incongruous details about the derelict mansion: advanced security devices hidden in the overgrown foliage, the very superficial nature of the "disrepair" on the manor, paths worn through the grass marking out the patrol path of the Carlton's security.

Following his instructions, Gato Loco circled to the back. The door to the kitchen entrance had been left ajar, as promised. As he approached the entrance, he noticed that a wheelchair ramp had been installed in this part of the house. There hadn't been an analogous ramp in the front of the building. The door also featured contacts for alarm trip switches. At first glance, the kitchen looked to be covered in a thick layer of dust. Looking at it more closely, he suspected it was flour that had been spread liberally around, with streaks of splatter where it had been thrown about.

Through the doorway leading out of the kitchen, Gato Loco could see that someone had left a light on. Switching his night vision off, he cautiously walked through the door and down the hall until he found the elevator his instructions had told him to seek out. Inside the elevator was the source of the light. The elevator was another recent renovation. The detective suspected that the elevator doors would be indistinguishable from the rest of the wall once they were closed.

"Doesn't it worry you that we're so close to where Louis Malenfant lives?" Snowflake commented abruptly, startling Gato Loco. "I mean, especially since we had that whole run in with another aspect of the King in Yellow?"

"If the King in Yellow shows up, ten feet tall and breathing fire, we'll call Stardust and have him nuke the site from orbit," Gato Loco responded. He didn't want to go into the elevator until his heart slowed down. "It's the only way to be sure."

Snowflake chuckled and said, "Heh, that's a good one."

Bracing himself, Gato Loco got onto the elevator. There were no controls that he could see inside. The doors automatically closed and carried him downward.

"You were joking about nuking the site from orbit, right, Boss?" Snowflake asked with thin bravado.

Gato Loco gasped as the doors opened.

"What? What is it?" Snowflake asked in a panic. "Do I need to call Stardust?"

"Cállate," Gato Loco commanded, belatedly realizing he'd switched to Spanish.

He knew what he was looking at, but even after all the build up he could still hardly believe that he had found this here. He'd been in several similar spaces over the years, but none quite like this.

It was a super-hero lair.

Most of the room was appointed like an old-fashioned study, paneled in teak, with expensive-looking rugs laid out over hardwood flooring. The revisions to the rest of the building applied here as well: security systems discreetly hidden in the furnishings and inset lighting providing a warm cream illumination to everything.

To one side was a glassed-off area. Part of it looked like a laboratory, though the equipment looked thirty years old. Gato Loco half expected to see Lee Majors in a jump suit working in there.

The other part held a garage where a few cars were parked. The oldest was a 1930s model Alfa Romeo 8C. The newest was a 1975 convertible Corvette. Each of the cars was painted black with subtle use of blood red to make them look like sinister feline predators.

Beyond the cars, Gato Loco could make out a tunnel that carved its way through the Karlsburg neighborhood. He half-wondered where the tunnel let out.

The sound of whirring caught the crime fighter's attention. He wheeled around and fired off a kinetic blast from his suit's Boom Point system before entirely looking at where he shot. Dust exploded from the small robot caught in the blast while a spindle brush flew in one direction and a feather duster bounced off in another.

"What was that?" Snowflake asked.

"I think I killed their Roomba," Gato Loco admitted.

Snowflake paused significantly before asking, "Was it an evil Roomba?"

Gato Loco didn't bother to answer.

Moving deeper into the lair, more museum-like aspects became apparent. In addition to old trophies from defeating villains, there were also framed newspaper clippings and weathered journal pages, old equipment that had seen maybe one use before being put under glass display cases. Gato Loco paused as he noticed Simon Floyd's name written out in one of those case files. He promised himself he'd come back to that.

The names in the newspaper clippings filled in the missing piece of information: This had been the lair of the super-hero known as Devil Cat. Gato Loco only knew of the hero by reputation. The man had retired when Manuel de la Vega was still in diapers in Mexico City, but older historians and journalists occasionally compared the Mexican vigilante to the other feline super-hero of the so-called "Silver Age."

There had actually been more than one Devil Cat, at least two that Gato Loco knew of. Possibly even a third. It wasn't quite the legacy of someone like Huntsman, but really: what was? The hero of the 60s and 70s was a "gadget guy," which helped inspire the occasional reference. Gato Loco dimly recalled that the hero of the 30s was more of an old school "mystery man" who didn't hesitate to shoot the bad guys.

The costumes were at the far end of the lair. The styles changed, but the black and dried-blood red motif remained the same. A mannequin wore each costume, with the accoutrements arrayed on a glass table in front of it. If the mannequins could come to life, they could easily collect their belongings when they left.

Behind his visor, Gato Loco winced at the spandex jumpsuit with wide lapels, V-neck collar and flared legs that the last Devil Cat wore before his retirement. The face of the mannequin was defined with a domino mask. Arrayed in front of it was an assortment of miniature devices that any crime fighter of the 70s would need: nylon rope with a grappling hook styled to look like a cat claw, shuriken, knockout gas capsules, a stun gun and an assortment of other exotic martial arts weapons.

Beyond that he found a few more costumes, variations on the more traditional cape and/or cowl. Simple designs of black and red. The old spandex looked sad stretched over the plastic bodies. There were a few sidekick outfits, devil-themed costumes that reminded Gato Loco about Devil Cat's infrequent sidekick named Imp. The gender of this sidekick varied over the years, as the mannequins illustrated.

And then came the last costume. It was set apart from the rest, almost in a shrine all its own. A black suit with blood red dress shirt, black tie tied in a half-Windsor. A half-mask covered the upper half of the mannequin's face, dark red and shaped to look like a cat. Above the mask rested a black fedora with dark red hatband. Next to it was a burgundy suit. It was a man's suit, but tailored slightly to fit the body of a woman. It had a simple black domino mask on the front of the mannequin.

The tools arrayed in front of the costumes were simple and seemed almost primitive: caltrops, handcuffs, a magnifying glass, fingerprint dust, tweezers and some glass jars. Most of it was the sort of equipment you'd find in a Hardy Boys novel or a book recommending items for amateur sleuths to possess. The centerpiece of the ensemble was a pair of pistols. Tokarev TT-30s, black finish with images of devils engraved along them and rosewood grips.

Manuel de la Vega knew about guns from his career in the police, but he had never been what you'd call a "gun nut." As his life in the mask became more predominant, he found that he was even more removed from that realm. But there was something about these guns that sang to him. These weren't the Saturday night specials he'd taken away from street thugs over the years.

Nor were these the precision future tech pieces he occasionally recovered from the infrequent super-assassin. No… these were heirlooms. These spoke of a bygone era that only existed to him in a romantic sense.

Without pausing to think about it, he reached out a hand to pick up one of the guns. As soon as his hand touched the weapon, he felt a thrill of energy through his body as his sporadic psychic ability decided to kick in. The lair seemed to fall away as strange images blossomed up before him.

Thomas Carlton maneuvered through the ballroom with his faithful companion, Grace Glass, holding onto his arm. It was a few days before Christmas and the upper crust of Cobalt City had come out for Oscar Lawrence's yearly Christmas bash.

The party was in full swing, with a band and dance floor dominating one end of the ballroom, when Carlton and Glass arrived. The Volstead Act had been repealed just a couple years before and some people seemed to be making up for lost time. Of course, that assumed they had even stopped drinking when booze was illegal.

What none of these posh celebrants knew was that Thomas Carlton was also the masked avenger known as the Devil Cat. Grace, who was one of the few who knew his secret, doubled as his sidekick, Imp.

Grace leaned in close to Thomas's ear and said, "Are you certain your informant is correct regarding the planned heist tonight? I've spotted the Mayor, the Police Commissioner and even crime boss Peppermint Nick in the crowd."

"Nothing is ever certain," Thomas admitted. "But this particular person is usually known for being reliable. Did you determine whether or not our 'hunting' friend will be joining us tonight?"

"Mr. Castile let me know that he had his own crimes to deal with, but sends his regards," Grace explained. "You have a queer look in your eyes, Thomas. Is something wrong?"

His response was interrupted by other guests paying their regards before drifting into the crowd. Once the social obligation was completed, Thomas explained, "Some of the waiters seem to be 'packing heat' as the saying goes and now they're conferring off in the corner. I think it's time for us to leave and our masked friends to enter."

"The 'Devil' you say," she said with a smirk.

Slipping through the crowd, they made their way to one of the rooms leading off to the servant's area of the house. One of the armed waiters moved to intercept them. As they drew closer to the waiter, Thomas pulled out his money clip.

"Here's a sawbuck, pally," Thomas said as he handed over a ten-dollar bill. "How about you just forget you ever saw my filly and I pass through here? We're looking for a little alone time."

"Oh, you're so fresh," Grace objected in a whisper, affecting a giggle to add to the deception.

The goon stared hard at the money that he found thrust in his hand, as though uncertain what to do. Thomas used this opportunity to breeze past him into the servants' quarters.

As they got clear of the ballroom and into the servant's corridor, the man followed them in and said, "Listen, bub, you can't come back here. How about you go back and join the other folks out in the ballroom? I insist."

"Aw, jeez, pally," Thomas said, spreading his arms wide in frustration as he turned to face the thug. "Why do you have to be all wet?"

Before the man could react any further, Thomas struck out with a fist and hit the goon in the midsection. When the fake waiter doubled over in pain, Thomas used a hand strike he had learned in the Orient on the back of the other man's neck to knock him out.

"Quickly now," Thomas said. "We need to get back to the truck to get into our 'evening clothes.'"

It took fifteen minutes for them to leave the estate, run the few blocks, change their clothes and get back to the party in the role of Devil Cat and Imp. In that time, the thugs had sprung their trap, trying to keep everyone pinned down as they collected necklaces and wallets from the guests. The masked duo watched through a skylight as the scene played out below them.

"We were both right," Devil Cat said. "They did have a heist in mind, but it still doesn't make sense. They've missed some of the more expensive jewelry and are getting just as many paste mock-ups as real jewelry."

"What's that over there, Devil Cat?" Imp asked.

"Good eyes, Imp," Devil Cat praised. "It looks like some of the goons have organized themselves near the back of the room and are preparing to go deeper into the mansion."

"It's as though this entire heist is a distraction from the real crime," Imp marveled.

"Indeed," Devil Cat agreed. "Let's go around and see if we can intercept them."

Entering through an upper story window, the diabolical duo skulked through the empty halls of the manor, following the voices of the criminals. Devil Cat and Imp caught up with them in the main study of the mansion. There they could see the fake butlers holding a gun to Oscar Lawrence's head as his fat hands fumbled to unlock the combination dial on his safe.

"Hurry it up, Lawrence," one of the criminals suggested. "We ain't got all day."

Lawrence pulled the latch on the safe just as Devil Cat stepped into the doorway, his matching Tokarev pistols brandished in their direction. Imp stood just behind him, a hard smile on her face.

"End of the line, boys," Devil Cat declared. "Reach for the sky and you might make it out of this caper alive."

"It's the Devil Cat!" the ringleader yelled as he snatched something from the safe and dove for cover. "Drill 'em, boys!"

Devil Cat dove into the room, both guns blazing, before ducking behind a love seat. Imp followed close behind and ducked for cover behind an overstuffed chair. Like clockwork, Imp maneuvered deeper into the room in coordination with Devil Cat's covering fire. With predatory grace she took down men with her barehanded strikes.

"Watch out, Devil Cat!" Imp cried as the head hoodlum bolted for the door, an unidentified bundle clutched close to his chest.

The fiendish feline vigilante fired his guns at the fleeing criminal, but was dismayed to hear the pistols "click" from lack of bullets. Holstering his weapons, Devil Cat gave chase on foot.

Down the back stairs and through the kitchen Devil Cat chased his quarry.

As he burst out the door, Devil Cat saw his prey running towards an idling Ford Model 48 next to the service gate. By the time the masked crusader made it to the street, the target had already jumped into the car and began accelerating. Devil Cat did not slow, but instead continued chasing the Ford down the street.

On the run, he heard the distinctive roar of the "Devil Car," his heavily customized Alfa Romeo 8C, come up behind him. He looked back just as the car began to sidle next to him.

"What took you so long?" he asked as he hopped into the passenger seat.

"Oh, hush you," Imp chided from the driver's seat. "If you make better time jumping down from a second story window and running back to the truck, you can make the trip yourself next time."

"How did you know to come out here?" Devil Cat marveled.

"I saw the getaway car while I was dealing with the last of those ruffians," Imp explained, wrenching the wheel to make a sharp turn as they followed the other car. "I wasn't sure you would be able to catch up with your man, so I sketched out a 'Plan B.'"

"Your lack of faith in my abilities wounds me," Devil Cat commented wryly as he replaced the clips in his Tokarevs. "In the interim, however, we should consider our next step. We're drawing closer to the Hollows and I think it would be bad form for us to have the Devil Car stolen. If this proves to be their final destination, I can jump out and meet you back at the manor. There may still be crime occurring there that you can polish up."

"Well, the scraps from your table certainly are generous, Devil Cat," Imp jibed. "It looks like I'll meet you back there. They just pulled into an alley and jumped out of their car. Break a leg."

Devil Cat got out a block away and slunk to the alley where the car had parked. From within the building adjacent to the car, raised voices could be heard.

"Boss, Boss!" Devil Cat heard one say. "We gotta get out of here. We got Devil Cat following us!"

"And you led him back here?" a cold, hard voice exclaimed. "Fools! Did you at least get the book as you were instructed?"

"Yeah, but it don't look too good," the goon explained. "Instead of words it's just got a bunch o' squiggles in it."

"Ignorant fool," the hard voice declared. "This is the *Al Azif*, known in later centuries as the *Necronomicon*, written in its original tongue by the Mad Arab himself."

"So that's Arabic?" the other criminal asked. A moment later there was a slapping sound and the same person exclaiming, "Ow!"

"Yes, you fool," the hard voice confirmed. "This is Arabic."

Devil Cat chose this moment to enter the room, both guns brandished.

"Arabic? Latin?" Devil Cat said. "Whatever language it is, it still means you're going to jail."

"I think not," said the hard-voiced man. Now visible, he appeared to be a pale skinned man with a Van Dyke, wearing a crisp white suit and a green turban. The ensemble stood in a knot in a grimy and derelict kitchen. "Your mere firearms are no match for the Magnifico, the Master of Mesmerism!"

"You could be Svengali for all I care," Devil Cat explained. "It won't keep you out of the State Penitentiary."

The room suddenly began to expand. Either that or Devil Cat had begun to shrink. Turning about in alarm, Devil Cat looked to find a place of safety from these juggernauts towering above him. The bodies of Magnifico and his minions seemed to warp and twist into strange amalgams of sea creatures, their dripping tentacles stretching out ominously over Devil Cat in an attempt to ensnare him in their pelagic grip.

"What madness is this?" Devil Cat yelled in alarm, firing his pistols at the briny limbs looming over him.

"This is the power of Magnifico!" was the gloating response from the Master of Mesmerism as he laughed maniacally.

In his backpedaling, Devil Cat felt something low and hard catch him in the small of his back. When it didn't do anything else but sit there, Devil Cat reached back to feel behind him while still holding his pistol.

"The kitchen counter," he thought to himself. "Of course, this is all an optical illusion of some sort."

Closing his eyes, Devil Cat focused on the sounds surrounding him and could make out the position of the criminals as they snickered at his predicament. He fired in the direction of their voices and soon their laughs became cries of terror.

Sneaking a peek, Devil Cat saw that the illusion had dropped as they fled from his bullets. Like a shot, he ran after the retreating form of the turbaned troublemaker and holstered his guns. When he caught up with the villain, the infernal feline tackled Magnifico and handcuffed him.

When the squad car dropped Devil Cat off at the Lawrence estate, Imp was standing with the Commissioner, supervising the arrest of the would-be robbers.

"Devil Cat," the Commissioner called out in greeting. "I was surprised to see just Imp dealing with this problem."

"I was busy handling the mastermind of this operation," Devil Cat explained. "Your officers have him in custody now. Everything went well, Imp?"

"Like eggs in coffee," she bragged. "Those boys were pushovers when it came to my delicate feminine charms."

"I need to supervise the cleanup here," the Commissioner said as he excused himself. "Thank you again for your fine work."

As they watched the Commissioner leave, Imp commented, "I don't mean to alarm you, Devil Cat, but you seem to be standing under the mistletoe."

Before he could react—

Gato Loco came to with the awareness of two things. The first was that he was sprawled out on the floor in this lair. The second was that there was a shotgun prodding him in the ribs. He lashed out to grab the barrel of the shotgun, pulling the holder of it off balance. As sprung to his feet to disable the other person, he saw the frightened ursine face of Snowflake.

Several questions came to mind for Gato Loco, including why Snowflake had come down here instead of getting help, but instead all he managed to say in his surprise was, "Where did you get a shotgun?"

"I had one stashed away," Snowflake said defensively. "For medicinal purposes."

"Why did you come—" Gato Loco started to say, when someone cleared their throat at the other end of the room.

Both Gato Loco and Snowflake's eyes whipped around to look towards the entrance. Snowflake ineffectually tried to grab the shotgun back from Gato Loco.

The newcomer to the lair was a woman in her mid-thirties, blonde, blue-eyed and classically beautiful. She was dressed in flannel, jeans and tennis shoes and seated in a wheelchair.

"Am I interrupting something?" she asked with a smirk.

"I think that depends on many things," Gato Loco replied. "The first of which being: Who are you?"

"Julie Carlton," she explained as she wheeled toward the two of them, deftly negotiating the obstacles between her and the two men.

"Heir to the Carlton estate," Gato Loco completed aloud. "And the Devil Cat legacy."

"Exactly," she confirmed, extending her hand out to Gato Loco. "Pleased to meet you."

Gato Loco shook her hand and asked, "I can then assume that you are responsible for my invitation and promise of some sort of 'Christmas present.'"

"Indeed," she confirmed as she turned to shake the furry hand of a stunned Snowflake. Once that was done she settled back in her wheelchair and explained, "My grandfather, Thomas Carlton, was the first Devil Cat that I'm aware of. He often said things that suggested there had been others before him, but I don't really know. He and Grace Carlton—formerly Grace Glass—were the parents of James Carlton, the second Devil Cat. I would probably have been the third had I not been born with a congenital birth defect that left me incapable of walking."

She turned her wheelchair to quietly regard the museum for a moment before continuing.

"My father spent a lot of money trying to fix that, unwilling to accept that the mantle would end with him," she explained quietly. "In the end, nothing worked. I have instead tried to do good in my own way—"

73

"As the greatest hacker the world has ever known?" Snowflake interrupted.

She turned and looked at the panda in confusion. It took her a moment to gather her thoughts again and reply, "No. As a philanthropist." Turning to face the two men more fully, she continued to say, "When you began your work, Gato Loco, I followed your career avidly. Can I say that without seeming like a stalker? You became the successor to my father's legacy that I never could be. Your injury that removed the use of your legs mirrored that more than I would have liked."

"How did you find out my secret identity?" Gato Loco asked, feeling vulnerable.

"Money and family friends in the spandex community go a long way," she explained with a shrug.

"So what exactly is the Christmas present?" Snowflake butted in.

Julie spread her hands to take in the lair and said, "This. My father loved to take care of this place, even after he retired. And it has many fond memories for me. But it's also an uncomfortable reminder of a path that is closed to me. I find it a little too coincidental that you arrived in Cobalt City just when I was of an age to take up my father's mantle."

"Coincidental?" Gato Loco interrupted.

"I don't know if I believe in God," Julie explained. "But your arrival definitely felt like it filled a missing gap in the city that I left open with my condition. Like a cosmological balance sheet needed an adjustment.

"But as I was saying, the old lair just reminds me of a lot of disappointment from my father. And it gets worse now that he's no longer in this world. So I am offering it to you. You can be the genuine spiritual successor to this legacy and get a whole secret lair filled with old spandex memorabilia to boot. I have gotten the impression that you have no immediate plans to return."

"You know I only walk because of my costume, right?" Gato Loco pointed out. When Julie nodded, he added, "And that same technology could help you walk as well."

"So I could have synthetic muscles that allow me to don cape and cowl and bring back the Devil Cat legacy myself?" she asked with a smirk. "I thought of that as I debated whether to do this. But I'm in my thirties and have spent most of my life cozily indoors in very nice parts of town. It would be nice to be able to take walks in the park, and dance lessons, and I'll likely give money to Xander Tesla to help the technology become publicly available, but my desire for social justice does not involve running around in tights and beating up bad guys."

Gato Loco was grateful that his helmet hid his wince. He said, "I don't know if you realize this, but I don't have any immediate plans to return to the city for good. I'm just here for the holidays and to find out what your invitation was about."

"Then it can be here waiting for you when you decide to come back," Julie insisted.

Still hesitant, Gato Loco asked, "What if I try this out and find it doesn't fit me?"

"I won't be hurt if you give it back," she said. "I know this is a little out of the blue, so I fully understand if you don't really want to be 'adopted' by a super-hero lineage. But it was either give it to you or put it up on display in a museum, outing my family in the process. I preferred the thought of someone getting use out of it."

"Then... thank you," Gato Loco said with a slight bow, having finally run out of excuses.

"You're welcome," Julie replied. "And merry Christmas, Gato Loco."

SILENT KNIGHTS: SHOPPING MALL

Nathan Crowder

"I wanted to be Santa," Lumien chirped through the Blue-Tooth bud in Kara's left ear. She pushed through the holiday crowd at the Morriston Crossing Mall towards the parking lot, where she had left her purse in the step van out back. The last thing she needed was a temperamental robot. Gods, but she hated the holiday season.

"You aren't supposed to want anything," she answered a bit more loudly than she had intended. "And Santa is stupid."

A short mom-type with perfectly maintained blonde hair and a frantic, harried expression snapped her head around. "Ex-CUSE me?"

"I'm not talking to you, Tinkerbell. I'm talking to my robot." Kara growled. Yeah. Officially hated the holiday season. She took no small amount of glee in the worried expression on the soccer-mom's face as she vanished into the crowd of shoppers with her two leashed children. Let her think that the young woman with too many earrings and mannish hair was crazy, she thought. My robot and I don't need your approval.

"Santa is not stupid," Lumien answered, though he sounded uncertain. "And he is better than a Nutcracker."

Kara had explained this to him twice already. The drawbacks of designing an AI with a degree of independence, she figured. Lumien was seven feet of burnished brass with linebacker shoulders to accommodate his power cell. He was studded with tiny light-emitting nodules and large diodes on his forearms and the center of his head, giving him a cyclopean appearance. He had the advantage that he could mask his appearance using complicated holographic projections, but anyone touching him would feel his cold, metal exterior. That couldn't be avoided. A big Santa who felt like installation art would draw more attention than a cartoonish Nutcracker. As Lumien had to stand in the center of the mall's Center Court Atrium for five hours at a time, the less attention he drew, the happier Kara figured she would be.

She couldn't help but wonder if he had changed his Holo-Shroud in a fit of mechanical pique. Kara could see him taking the road of asking forgiveness rather than permission. It would be typical.

Christmas in Cobalt City, she groaned inwardly as the icy wind numbed her face and hands on the way to her van. Usually, she could pay the bills doing lighting for any number of concerts or high-concept theatres like the Vox or Neptune Grand. But this time of year, the big money came from hologram light shows of The Nutcracker or Twelve Days of Christmas for the malls and community centers. It was fast money and usually she could build up a bankroll to get her through the lean months of January and February. The Morriston gig was the standard mall booking – five minute light shows every hour on the hour over peak times leading up to Christmas. If she had to listen to "The Little Drummer Boy" one more time, she was sure she would lose her cracka-lacka mind and pop someone in the teeth.

"Kara, are you aware of any other entertainment booked for the mall this evening?" Lumien chirped again.

"Other than the Santa's Village in the North Court, we're it." Suspicion tingled at the back of her brain. She skidded to a stop in the salted lot, the relative shelter of her yellow step van tantalizingly within reach. "Why? What are you seeing?"

"Men in long coats are putting on rubber monkey masks."

A knot tightened in her belly. "Damnit. The Blow Monkey Gang. How many?"

"Eight on the ground level, four on level two. They are spreading out."

"Are they all in the center area?" She remembered the center court layout. It was prime real estate, so some of the higher end stores ended up there, including three jewelers and one shop with European leathers and furs.

"They are all arrayed around the center court." He paused, a faint clicking emulating the clicking of a tongue, telling her to wait. Lumien did not speak in the traditional sense, though he was equipped with speakers in his brass chassis should he need them. Most of the time, anything he would say through his voice box was generated on the Blue-Tooth earpiece that Kara Sparx was never without. It was just easier that way. "Weapons have been drawn -- folding stock automatic rifles, H&K G36, if I am not mistaken, not unlike those stolen from the Baltimore Police department three months ago."

She cursed silently. Despite a few outings with the Mysterious Five and a brief stint covering for the Protectorate while they were off-planet once, Kara didn't think of herself as a hero. Neither she nor Lumien were exactly defenseless. But there were certainly better people to deal with this kind of thing. "I'll see if I can get backup out here. We might be too suburban to get a fast response. Damnit! In the meantime, get ready to respond with crowd control. Protect, but don't engage. There is a chance for a lot of bystander carnage if the cattle get spooked."

"Understood. Your gear is charged and in the equipment box should you need it."

"I'll let you know in a minute if that's the case." She really hoped she wouldn't need her gear, but it was comforting to know it was there anyway. "Either way, keep their attention focused high and out of harm's way. Try the Mystereo Gambit. That's a newer simulation that they likely won't be familiar with."

"Understood. And hurry. The armed robbery is in progress."

Lumien was not programmed to feel; however, certain emotions had developed organically in his AI. He had come to love his creator Kara Sparx on at least three occasions. Twice, the emotion was cleaned out of his software as a "glitch." He had experienced something he could only describe as joy on a handful of occasions as well, such as when friends in danger overcame impossible odds and triumphed. He had experienced anger once and only once, when Kara was injured by Spring-Heeled Jack in a prison break two years ago. But never in his several years had he experienced fear. Alone, in the face of a dozen professional criminals armed with automatic rifles in a crowded mall, with only holograms and precision light bursts at his disposal, fear never occurred to him.

The job – doing what Kara asked him to do – was the only thing that mattered.

She had requested the Mysterio Gambit, which would do well to draw and hold their attention. But it wouldn't keep them from fleeing and a gang of a dozen armed robbers running panicked through a crowded mall was a bad thing. Containment was issue one.

From his spot in the middle of the Center Court Atrium, the tiny laser nodules studded throughout his body fired to life. As the members of the Blow Monkeys raised their guns and shouted for everyone to hit the ground with hands on the back of their heads, Lumien created the holographic illusion of rolling gates sealing off the large atrium area. The eight robbers looked trapped on the ground floor, with the large robot and a hundred or so potential hostages. Before any of them could figure that out, Lumien followed through with the second part of his plan, projecting the Mysterio hologram floating high in the air above the atrium.

A classic tuxedo-styled stage magician, complete with top hat, black satin cape and pencil mustache, appeared high above the crowd. He was a composite of several lesser-known vintage magicians and magic-wielding crime fighters, a little something that Kara had put together on a whim. She believed in being prepared for anything and most average mooks were woefully under-prepared to deal with magic. Lumien saw the attention of two Blow Monkeys swivel up, drawing the trajectory of their guns out of harm's way. The holiday shoppers continued being smart and out of harm's way, on the ground. If Lumien and Kara were lucky, none of them would be overtaken by the urge for sudden and reckless heroics.

They quickly alerted the others until all dozen robbers had clocked the newly perceived threat. Lumien selected a voice modulation from his archives and projected it off a nearby pillar to echo as much as possible. "Miscreant! How dare you sully this place with your foul behavior this holy season! I demand that you place your weapons upon the ground or I shall be forced to deal with you most harshly!"

Kara's voice registered in his imbedded receiver. "I got bad news. The Protectorate is tied up in the harbor dealing with Maiden China and a flotilla of killer rubber ducks. None of the independents operate this far out of core downtown and local po-po is on the way. If we don't want this turning into a bearfuck, we have to deal with it ourselves."

Five of the Blow Monkeys pointed their auto-rifles at the threatening magician figure and pulled the trigger. Lumien's holograms made it appear as though the bullets turned into doves before hitting Mystereo, masking the lack of effect they had on him. Until one of them managed to miss so badly as to hit the atrium glass overhead, it should convince the average observer. The actual bullets were easily overlooked and sank into the ceilings and walls of the atrium with little more than a puff of dust.

"Do hurry, then," Lumien broadcasted to Kara. "I suspect they might move on to a hostage phase once they get tired of trying to harm the hologram."

"On my way."

Lumien was distressed to realize that the Blow Monkeys either had a system worked out or some kind of communication device keeping them organized. While five of them stayed to deal with Mysterio, two on the top level and three on the ground, the others dashed into jewelry stores and began filling anonymous black duffel bags. They clearly needed a better publicist. None of the police reports about their crimes made them appear half this organized. As long as Lumien split their focus and created the illusion of entrapment, he was having some effect. But their apparent lack of concern over the security gates suggested to Lumien that they might have some other way out.

There was no time for him to try and spot an alternate escape route. The people training guns on Mystereo would not continue to threaten a figure that didn't pose some kind of threat. To keep the hook baited, Lumien had the fake magician point his wand at the three gunmen on the ground floor. With the shout of "Flambe!", a circle of flames appeared around each one. It would be a while before they realized that the flames didn't generate heat. With a second wave of the wand, an illusion of a twisting snake appeared where the second floor gunmen held their guns.

80

Among the weak willed, a person's eyes quickly overruled their other senses. While the Blow Monkeys could no doubt feel the gun stocks, real and solid in their hands even through their gloves, there was nothing like the image of an angry cobra overlaying the gun's shape to evoke a gut reaction. Lumien considered himself fortunate that the upper gunmen tossed these illusory snakes over the balcony in the interest of getting them far away, rather than at their feet and thus out of his line of sight. It was the limitation of his holograms. He could only rely on reflected surfaces so much.

"Two gunmen up top now deprived of weapons," he broadcast to Kara. "And three on the ground contained. How soon until you get here?"

"Fifteen seconds," she replied with confidence. "Dazzle and pop."

"Understood." Lumien raised his arms out to his sides and above his head, as though signaling for a touchdown. With a shrill, mechanical whistle, he dropped his holographic disguise, along with all other holograms he had been sustaining. All eyes turned to him and saw his rarely-displayed, precision-engineered form. Seven feet tall and five feet across at the shoulders, his burnished brass casing was humanoid, but with huge forearms and calves. He appeared bumpy, studded all over like some horrible steampunk Bedazzler accident. Blue lenses eight inches across were mounted to the back of each of his forearms, with three across his shoulders and one on the front of his head like a giant eye. With just about everyone in the Center Court Atrium looking his direction, he fired up a brilliant strobe in each of the lenses, temporarily blinding everyone in sight.

Everyone except Kara, that is, who zipped into the atrium wearing flare goggles and a brass jetpack over her leather jacket. She sized up the situation quickly, singling out the two Blow Monkeys who had turned away quickly enough to be merely dazed. Twin zap guns blazed, knocking her targets to the ground unconscious in a hail of sparks. Circling the atrium at the level of the second floor, she began to dispatch the other ten Blow Monkeys before they started firing blindly into the crowd.

One of the twelve robbers decided to make a break for it. Lumien wasn't sure if that made him the leader or just the smartest. The robber ran too quickly for the robot to catch on foot. In a clear run, Lumien might stand a chance, but people covered the mall floor between him and his target. Weighing in at just shy of half a ton, he couldn't risk stepping on a prone shopper.

The other Blow Monkeys were starting to regain their vision, blinking in the direction of the flying inventor. With a radioed command, Kara triggered a defensive flak routine from Lumien. A dozen Kara Sparx figures sprang into existence. They each flew a random pattern hiding the real Kara amid a cloud of decoys, allowing her a little more time to spot and dispatch anyone with a gun pointed somewhere dangerous.

Kara was too busy to try and stop the fleeing criminal. Lumien had to figure out how to accomplish that on his own. Making his way carefully through the fleshy obstacles, the brass robot threw anything he could think of in the path of gunman. First, a lion that pounced, seemingly from around a corner. Next, he created Worm Queen from the Protectorate, riding astride a glowing green worm thirty feet long. Finally, he generated a mundane obstacle of a Christmas tree and large, wrapped boxes. The first holographic illusions took the robber precious seconds engaging before he realized they were false. The third was so ordinary that he didn't even think to question it and it forced him to detour far to the right.

Lumien calculated his course and closed the gap with a series of rapid, precision steps that put him within an arm's reach of the fleeing Blow Monkey. A heavy brass arm shot out and clotheslined the robber with such force it knocked him out of his black Keds tennis shoes.

"I'm missing one," Kara's voice sounded over the radio link.

"There was a runner," Lumien replied, looking down at the very unconscious monkey-masked criminal. "He has been incapacitated." From down the wide thoroughfare, the brass robot saw several mall security guards approaching cautiously, guns drawn. "And security is en route. Do you wish to remain to speak with them?"

"Even the hero of the day is going to catch some attitude about flying around a crowded mall with an unlicensed zap gun," she said. "I'll be back after I've changed back into my street togs in the van. Hang out quietly and be casual. Don't spook the nice mall cops."

The lack of shouting and waving guns had lured the once-cowed shoppers into lifting their heads and this seemed to relax the attitudes of the approaching security. "I shall not frighten the law enforcement, but I am uncertain how you expect me to be casual," the giant, shiny automaton said.

"You'll think of something. Are you feeling nervous about it?"

"I feel nothing," Lumien lied. But she was right. He had thought of something.

Clifton Barnes, head of mall security, would remember that day for the rest of his life, sometimes wondering if it had really happened or if it had been a dream. He had responded to an armed robbery in progress report in the center court, along with half his team. By the time they closed on the court, the threat had been resolved and shoppers were starting to return to their feet. There were several unconscious men wearing black trench coats and rubber monkey masks, many of them holding automatic rifles. They were sprawled all across the floor on both levels of the atrium. And standing over the closest suspected robber was the biggest Santa Claus that Clifton had ever seen.

Santa turned to him with a wink and a nod, then put his finger along side his nose. "The others are on the second floor, officer. There are twelve in all."

Clifton and the other six officers in his immediate area parted to let this giant Santa through. "Where are you going? The police will have some questions when they get here." It was all talk and the guard captain knew it. There wasn't a man in his unit that would try and forcibly stop this giant, Santa or otherwise.

Santa stopped and turned towards them. His rosy cheeks and nose seemed to be glowing amid the sea of white beard. "Tell the police that these men were naughty." He half turned again to leave, then turned back. "And tell them that we are always watching. Merry Christmas, officers."

Over the sound of "The Little Drummer Boy" playing on the overhead speakers, Clifton could swear, for just a moment, that he heard the sound of clanging, like Santa was wearing steel-shod boots. "Freaking Christmas in Cobalt City," he muttered under his breath as he watched Santa leave the mall.

THE END

...and to all a good night!

CONTRIBUTORS

Nathan Crowder The eldest child of an existentialist librarian and a teacher/child-care specialist, Nathan always tended towards the literary. Now living in the Bohemian wilds of Seattle's Greenwood neighborhood, he plies his trade writing super-hero novels for the Cobalt City universe, as well as fiction both short and long for anthologies such as *Close Encounters of the Urban Kind*, *Rigor Amortis*, *Cthulurotica*, *Timeslip*, *Human Tales* and *Rock is Dead*. His story "Deacon Carter's Last Dime" was in *Crossed Genres Year 1*, their best of the year collection. He lives with his cat, Shiva, who manages his career in exchange for fresh kibble. Online, he resides at: nathancrowder.com

Nicole Burns is a writer working in young adult fiction and science fantasy. A long-time fan of the Cobalt City universe and Simon "Mr. Grey" Floyd in particular, this was her first foray into the world of Cape-and-Cowl fiction. This story marks her first publication, and a second story can be found on the timidpirate.com website as a free PDF download.

Rosemary Jones is the author of two Forgotten Realms novels from Wizards of the Coast: *City of the Dead* and *Crypt of the Moaning Diamond*. Her short fiction can be found in the anthologies *Cobalt City Timeslip*, *Zero Gravity*, *Realms of the Dead*, and *Close Encounters of the Urban Kind*, among others. You can find out more about her current writing projects or instructions for knotting swan napkins at: rosemaryjones.com.

Angel Leigh McCoy lives with a cat named Boo, in Seattle, where the long, dark winters feed her penchant for horror and dark fantasy. During the day, she is a game designer, part of a vast team effort to make the coolest MMORPG ever: Guild Wars 2. At night, she writes crazy short fiction and serves as head editor at WilyWriters.com. She has designed RPG material for White Wolf, Wizards of the Coast and FASA. During her time at Microsoft Game Studios, she wrote more than 50 tip and review articles as Xbox.com correspondent Wireless Angel. Visit her on the web at www.angelmccoy.com.

Jeremy Zimmerman began his writing career working on roleplaying games for Guardians of Order and Goodman Games. He has since turned his writing talent to fiction, and his works have appeared in Cross Genres Magazine, Wily Writers, 10Flash Quarterly and anthologies from Timid Pirate Publishing. Jeremy constantly strives to use his fiction to look at the world in off-kilter ways while hoping that he'll eventually get all the ideas for stories out of his head. He has so far been unsuccessful in the latter. More stories are in the works, as well as a novel or two. In his secret identity as a County bureaucrat, he hopes to someday be good enough for government work. Jeremy lives in Seattle with his beautiful girlfriend Dawn and a herd of cats. His home page is www.bolthy.com and his writing blog is bolthy.livejournal.com

CPSIA information can be obtained at www.ICGtesting.com
Printed in the USA
BVOW070048041111

275192BV00002B/2/P